Crossings 42

Animals

ANIMALS

Sofia Pirandello

BORDIGHERA PRESS

Translation by Contextus, Pavia, Italy.

Cover art features a photograph by the author.

Library of Congress Control Number: 2024944553

Published by
BORDIGHERA PRESS
John D. Calandra Italian American Institute
25 W. 43rd Street, 17th Floor
New York, NY 10036

Crossings 42
ISBN 978-1-59954-225-6

TABLE OF CONTENTS

A mia nonna, la nostra Torre.
A chi ha il coraggio di ricordare, restare e resistere.
E a mio zio Pino, perché anche
le decorazioni hanno la loro importanza.

Not even the keenest among [caterpillars] could have imagined it was destined to become a butterfly. It is the same with us. What more do we know of our destiny than of our origins?

—JULIEN OFFRAY DE LA METTRIE

SUMMER

The first memory I have of myself is yellow. Just four years old and sitting on the soft, damp ground, I've picked a ripe lemon. I turn it over in my hands, fascinated by its bright color; a magnificent fruit ripe for cutting, not a trace of green on its surface. A cold sun, like a precious gem that's all mine. I lift it to my nose and try to capture its flavor, confined in a bitter, wrinkled skin. Blinding light all around and the incessant song of the cicadas. Several fields from home, alone for a few hours with myself and my lemon. I bring it even closer to my face and say, smiling, "You're beautiful." I know it understands me and swells with pride. Absorbed in reality, I'm able to feel happy. I'm just a little girl with a gorgeous lemon in her hands, everything is simple and fresh. Every leaf on every plant, the wind in my hair, the ants crossing the bridge made by my ankles in the soil ... it's all animated, alive, and it speaks to me. A brief shred of peace, then my mother's shrill voice calling me, tearing me away from my game. She wants me with her again. My dress is filthy, my mood suddenly black. I was born with a past, a mass of painful memories, a conscience. With just a handful of years under my belt, my eyes are deep black, flashing at the center like a pinpoint. After a while, I no longer hear my mother shouting, my father finds me and picks me up, holding me tight. He winks at me and pokes the dimple on my cheek, identical to his. "Let's not upset her, Luci'," he says, serious now, and we go home, hanging on to each other.

*

I was born in a sun-scorched village in Southern Italy. I don't remember a single winter in my childhood. My land is covered in dust and heat. The heat was everywhere: in the streets, in the air, at home. Heat on our skin, heat on our animals and among the olive trees, heat in the throats of the lizards and cicadas. Everything was scorched, straw-colored, our houses and our heads. My mother went crazy from the heat, the wind blowing it forcefully into her ears, sweeping away her thoughts and filling her head with dirt and hay. In the end, her head must have looked like the road outside our door.

My mother. Remembering my mother requires an effort. My mother visits me in my dreams, sometimes just her hands—spare, hysterical, convulsed, always busy—even cursing. My mother, the crazy woman.

The beginning is always the mother and the land.

Anna, my mother, was pretty. Anna means "grace"—a singularly inappropriate name that my mother wore without respect, without embodying its meaning. Dark is her curly and unruly hair and face, tall, slender, and shapely. Yet she would brush her hair and dress specifically to deemphasize her womanly curves. She loved to make herself ugly, to make herself nothing. She experienced shame for every excess filth, for vanity, for beauty, the inseparable companion of sin. Always dressed in mourning though I couldn't understand why, she would make for herself high-necked, shapeless dresses that looked old as soon as she put them on. Once I came across her remaking, with nervous hands, a job that had taken her weeks from scratch, because when she tried on the finished dress it fit her perfectly around the hips. Unbearable. She burst into tears, hit herself on the forehead repeatedly and ripped out all the seams with nervous hands. The sound of ripped fabric wounded my ears, imprinting a deep anguish in my chest.

Mama often used to say that the only things she couldn't forgive Our Lord for were having made her *fimmina*, a female, because from childhood this had only caused her trouble and left her exposed; and having doubled the pain by foisting a daughter on her. She would talk to herself, repeating that women are always prey, that they're weak.

Her fragile nerves, her dependence, and her loneliness were female, they were Our Lord's cruelty toward her. A woman has no desires, she has no strength, no hunger. My mother was none of these things, and she felt like she'd been punished for this. With every fiber of her being, she tried to adapt to the idea of what she should have been, tirelessly collecting failure after failure. After meals where she'd barely swallowed a crust of bread, she'd often hide away in the bathroom to eat, thinking that none of us knew. But I noticed her grasping hands, the few times we could afford something tastier to sink our teeth into. A woman has no appetite, she's always full, she cooks only for others.

Whenever she looked at me, she was ashamed she hadn't been able to keep one of her children from her own, terrible fate. I had no choice but to disappoint her, for the simple fact of existing, of having come after my brother. She recognized her own dark eyes in mine; something she couldn't stand. She would repeat metallically that she'd often prayed for a miscarriage when she was pregnant, purposely lifting too-heavy things so as to put an end to my presumption. She'd say this to hurt me, since she couldn't have known that I'd be a *fimmina* like her. Maybe, of course, she was afraid I would be. I was brazen, she'd say, you're sturdy and determined, she told me—disappointed—every day we spent together. On my part, I'd try translating her words so they'd seem strong but tender, the way I wished she'd speak to me. I was little, but hard, just as hot inside and on the surface. I held out, loving her despite myself.

I lived on the margins, both at home and beyond. When you're the child of a crazy mother in a tiny village, you'll never be more than a crooked plant, the anxious fruit of an uncertain nature, a promise of some future disaster, be it in her eyes or in everyone else's. The whole area had excluded us, leaving us on the outskirts and continuing to build further and further away from our patch of dark earth. Life, the future, raced away in the opposite direction, discarding us and leaving us standing in the dust and at its mercy. Although we lived near the sea, whenever I try to remember, all I see is dust, sweat, and solitude; we lived in a desert. The howling of the dogs the only subconscious signal of the presence of others. Even inside, the house we lived in was bare on account of our great poverty and my mother's obsessions;

from her I learned that you never really need anything that's not strictly necessary, life is life even reduced to bare bones, to the absolute center of things, with no rouge, makeup, or colors. Life, plain and simple, is enough. Our house was a hostile, dark cubicle—especially during our scorching summers, when the shutters had to stay closed to leave the heat outside. We fooled ourselves into thinking we could live in clean yet cramped rooms, forced to repeat day after day the useless motions of one who chases dust on an island of dry dirt. An ugly table and a few rough chairs, a couple of beds and a wardrobe, and not much more, that was it. The only luxuries we owned were the magnificent tablecloths and other lace things sewn by my mother. All you had to do was watch her working shaking with impatience in order to understand that such meticulous work was a punishment for her, which would soon fall to me, as well.

Only the brave live like this, and Christ loves them, my mother would say, and she was right. My childhood was a lifetime ago, another life, exceptionally hard, a life for those who are bold, with never a deception nor hope.

*

Our father was often away, for long periods as well. He'd go off in search of a better job, which would give us more *piccioli*, more money. He felt the heat in his stomach; he was always restless. He always wanted to change things, to be different—from the others and himself, from the man he'd been just a few days or hours before. The main thing was to have a mind of your own, to never bow to anyone. He even converted to Protestantism in order to choose his own religion. For the sake of changing, pure and simple, and to drive my mother even more crazy: It was a huge scandal in a village where religion isn't something you just change.

Of course, both my mother's craziness and our isolation were at least partly my father's fault. When they were just kids, he had convinced her that they should get married and build a family of their own. Despite being repeatedly rejected by her parents (which likely only increased his motivation), Papa convinced Mama to elope. She never would have wanted that, getting married isn't something to be done like thieves, in the shadows. It shouldn't start off like something wrong. The truth is, Mama was terrified of giving herself to a man. Everything had been easy with him until then; he'd given her back some peace. She'd been able to deceive herself into thinking there was nothing physical about a love affair, no guilt or shame. Now he wanted her, he was carrying her away, planting her somewhere else. Mama found herself facing the undeniable fact that Papa was greedy and selfish, a man like any other. She chose to play the part of the victim, with the deliberate intention of spiting someone, who knows who. They eloped, in classic style, on a dark and moonless night to get married in a tiny church that didn't welcome them as they'd hoped. The priest lit a single candle for them, which was all they deserved, and married and blessed them reluctantly, wishing the new couple to be bathed in a stronger light—the divine one—while secretly hoping for the opposite. He blew out the flame, which took with it as it went out a fragment of Anna's mind . From then on, they remained in the dark. Anna became convinced that no one should feel, no one should see matters of the heart.

Papa's domineering severed Mama's ties with her family and with the rest of the village, exposing her to nasty gossip. His unreliability and indecisiveness left her alone with two children to raise while she was still trying to find herself, prey to her past and memories, and to the restlessness that would so often shake her.

My grandfather, already a widower, couldn't bear it and took his own life, as his mother and sister had done many years before, seizing the first opportunity to avoid the hassle get out of the middle of everything, responding to a call that had always tempted him while simultaneously making a grand dramatic gesture. Entertaining the idea of death: a vocation and an instinct coming from the mother's side, my own personal torment. Some families have suicide in their blood, when you have the thought written deep down inside, you spend your whole life trying to drive it out. It's reassuring to know that there's always a way out: if worse comes to worst, you can decide you've seen enough. Personally, I've decided: suicide will never get me. It's good to have it just in case; I've reduced it to a screw screwed right into my temple, a constant companion, a sweet and melancholy thought that makes my face look pretty because it turns my smile downwards. I never had the chance to meet my grandfather, nor the women in my family, they decided not to wait for me. Dead or alive, they couldn't be by my side.

In the blood flowing through my body is written a formula that makes me resemble all these women, especially my great-aunt; I realized it from the few sepia portraits we kept of her. I bear some indecipherable facial trait that I've never been able to identify but makes us so alike. Maybe that's why I can feel that when she cut her wrists to die, she wasn't seeking the darkness and the cold of the stone. They found her with her eyes wide open and awake, until the very end frantically searching for some kind of happiness. She wasn't crazy, I've never believed that. She couldn't wait long enough, she was just tired.

They said that my grandfather had been unable to bear the wound to his pride, that my mother was a messed-up degenerate. Compassion is the most valued quality in a child, my mother had none for her old father. The entire village began thinking of her the same way as a murderer, as if she had killed him with her bare hands. Mama started to believe it, recognizing in herself an evil that inevitably went back to her feminine nature.

*

Sometimes Papa would disappear for days, until we'd find him there again, at the door of the house, ready to suggest new odd ideas to earn more, to be happier. He started by raising and selling chickens. Sometimes, when Mama was angry and wanted to spite him, she'd steal a few animals to make pillows out of them: she'd pull their necks violently and then pluck them. I'd watch their eyes pop, the beast's and my mother's—him desperate, her furious. They were the best days, ending with a hearty meat soup and a soft sleep.

Then my father got fed up with chickens. He decided to sell candy on street corners, another enterprise that lasted only a few weeks. With each new job, the whole family took on a new role, new duties, a new daily life. My brother and I had to follow him in his ventures, per

Mama's wishes. Mama always spoke in the plural about everything about Papa, his work and the family, and she expected my brother and I to do the same. She reluctantly let us go to school, counting the days until the end of our compulsory schooling. She held her breath until then, driven more by a natural respect for the law than by what was right for us.

Though we had to spend mornings at school, the afternoons belonged to Papa, they were family time. I was scolded and punished more than once for doing my homework. The same thing had happened to my older brother, and so we quickly learned to not even touch our books, pens, pencils, and paper in front of our mother, who would otherwise break our cheeks with the force of her blows. Reading terrified my mother especially, she was afraid it would make us stupid, confining us to idleness and immobility. We were to learn only the bare necessities to not go beyond what was allowed. Too many ideas clutter the mind and have never made anyone rich, let alone happy. So that's how I'd spend my afternoons: handing out chickens or candy, running errands, toting sacks with mysterious contents, and managing Papa's finances, which was an easy job, luckily, because if there were few expenses, the income was even less.

*

As for me, even before learning to read I had a great aversion to books: it felt like grownups were pranking me, I couldn't believe that all those *curiusi* marks inside books actually meant something. Later on, my mother's behavior would confirm that these objects were things one should not trust. A strange twist of fate, however, made me good at writing. I started to keep a diary where I jotted stuff down, at times summarized in a single word: *fatigue*, *play*, often *hunger*. When I was already writing fluently, at around eight years old, the teacher insisted on speaking with my mother. Alarmed, Mama brought me with her.

"Your daughter writes, ma'am."

"I'll punish her *pissubito*, right away. I'm very sorry."

"No, I mean your daughter writes well. Her words are like nails, driven right to the point."

It was stupid of him, I wished he'd never spoken. With just a few words he took away from me what he had wanted to give me.

My mother turned to me. She was as pale as if they'd accused her daughter of being a thief. You like to write?, she asked me. But what do you write? "Nails." That word had made her completely lose control. I didn't answer,

"*Nenti scrive mi figghia,*" hissed my mother, to save the family honor. "My daughter doesn't write anything."

There followed a death threat and a curse, and then my mother dragged me home, starting to slap me long before we got through the door. She said that sometimes the people who love you don't use gentle and smooth words but instead slap your soul out of you. I'm punishing you because it will help you, because I love you. School was for learning the bare minimum to help Papa, certainly not to jabber on about our business or, worse, to say things that shouldn't even be thought.

It was never spoken of again; I forced myself to hold my pen, the teacher his tongue. I made my words stupid and docile, almost like drawings or decorations. Pages filled with daisies and bows, random thoughts on the village boys who ran under my nose. I didn't really care about them, nor were they – busy in childlike affairs – interested in me. One thing I did know: I was supposed to like *masculi*, boys, yet also keep them at a safe distance. They were beautiful and dangerous, like the flames dancing in the fireplace. If you let them, they would take what they thought was theirs, and even more. Thus, the advice was to fear them without understanding them, so as not to get burned before I had to, something I thought would have repercussions on my worth and on that of everyone I cared about. Fascinated by such a catastrophic power, I envied it and wondered: my father and brother, were they *masculi* too?

I kept on writing my sharp but well-disguised words in a corner of a sheet of paper, or after a innocent lovelorn sigh. I was supposed to learn from normal children how to be one of them: a normal child. Yet I wasn't able to, despite my efforts. I had trouble connecting with my classmates, I wouldn't have wanted to be like them for all the world. A *fimmina*. I knew, because I'd heard people talk about it often, of some emotion called friendship, but I never actually felt it. I remained apart from them, like oil and water. Dense, rich, and golden, I was surrounded by silly girls with no special qualities or aspirations of any kind. Bright and empty, mirrors ready to reflect anything. Loving didn't cross the threshold of our home, it fluttered about our rooms, constantly rejected by my mother and by my brother. It leaned easily on my father.

I didn't love to study, but I was smart and knew it. In the same way I was disgusted by the children who studied to get recognition, who struggled to reach the point where I was already moving nimbly, and by the ones who didn't understand anything, who, too shy or too stupid, couldn't find the words to ask the teacher questions. Yet I was supposed to learn from them. No one in my village, except maybe the teacher, was ready to hear what was in my head. Writing poured out of me; inside me, I lovingly nursed my thoughts and started speaking less and less. I kept my diary of words in a safe place, hidden from view.

I had to move it once, my treasure had been unearthed and defaced. On the twenty-seventh of September of a year that has remained unspecified, the word *HAM*, in huge unsteady letters, dominates a white page. My diary had been read and disfigured, contaminated. My brother had decided to contribute to the collection of my thoughts. Enraged, I was tempted to destroy the notebook, following my mother's example; she would punish herself in order to teach others a lesson, perhaps overestimating the power of guilt. In the end, I decided that I couldn't live without that collection of words, the only proof of my true inner movements, a detailed and essential record of the impression the world left upon me. I looked for a more secure hiding place, safe from the ridicule that my brother, who never took himself too seriously, carried around with him.

My mother hasn't been with us for many years, now. But if she was right and there's something waiting for each of us after we die, now, wherever she is, she'd surely be happier to have a daughter who's thief or a murderer than a writer. The only things to be proud of are the ones you earn through hard work and the sweat of your brow, that you take care of with your own hands the way you tie complicated knots, even if it means killing a man. Moreover, I've always suspected that her hatred for herself and for me, for *all* women, actually concealed a deeper hatred for a man, who knows which man, who had burned her too early and against her will, who had taken her nerves by tearing them out like weeds, and who didn't deserve either anonymity or freedom. One less man on the face of the Earth can't do much harm, now that Mama has earned her place in heaven it's not a sin for her to think so.

*

Dad left again, for the last time. He went far away, to earn more *piccioli*, to make us all happy—everyone except my mother. He went first to Tobruk and then to Benghazi, where he finally got a job with the Civil Engineering Corps. One evening Mama gathered my brother and me together and solemnly informed us that our father had been militarized. None of us, not even her, knew what that really meant. I imagined him dressed like Charlemagne, my brother thought he was an pilot. At night, my mother dreamed of him in uniform, handsome as ever, at home with us.

He was made a prisoner of war, as if he were a soldier, *s'assintu mau*,[1] took ill, and died in a damp room from untreated pneumonia. He probably died in a place as hot as our area in the South, perhaps even hotter. They told us he had been buried like a general in the Italian military shrine of El Alamein, but we'd have much rather he come back to us as a chicken farmer or to sell candy. Little of him was returned to us: his pass for the colonies; his identity card (with the photo torn off); his wedding ring, which smelled terribly of iron because my parents had donated the original gold one to their homeland; a notebook full of accounts at a loss and of various passages of the Bible; a battered rosary, still warm from his prayers; some letters addressed to us that we never received.

His letters, moldy in the corners, always started the same way. "Dear Annuccia," wrote Papa, "I pray the Lord that this finds you in excellent health, together with our dear children." First, on February 8, 1942, our poor father had informed us that he had been taken prisoner.

---

1   "He got sick."

He insisted on reassuring us that he was, however, in good health and that we shouldn't worry about him, as he was being treated with great care by the "English gentlemen." We would also continue to receive his salary, which would be sent directly to our home. Benghazi wouldn't abandon us. Papa was sparing in details about his daily life, but curious about how things were going without him in our sweltering village. He had always been far away, but free. Imprisonment was clearly the only time he felt a real distance, and separation. In which he lived with longing and deprivation. Desperate from the lack of answers, Papa blithely kept writing us letters, in which he admitted that he knew at paper and ink were a heavy expense, especially for a family like ours. All the same, he begged his Annuccia to send news, even just occasionally, to soothe his heart. Concerned about our future, he revealed in one of the last letters that he had saved some money for my brother's and my education. Papa wasn't interested in our educational level, but he knew we needed a "piece of paper" to become someone. Specifically, he wished for a military career for my brother, he wanted him in uniform just as we had imagined Papa from afar. For me, on the other hand, he had planned a future as a teacher, "the only respectable job proper for a good girl in these modern times of ours." From the very first letters, moreover, he asked my mother, often and firmly, to make up her mind to move, once and for all, especially since he might never return. He thought it wasn't right for a woman to live so isolated, in a poorly frequented neighborhood, alone with two children. He hinted at the presence of someone whom he had never liked, as she well knew, and that it was time to leave. My mother, poor and alone, and with her weak nerves, must always remember: "Annuccia, the world is slime."

Papa had only finished the third grade, yet he made the effort to express himself accurately, with simple, clean, and elegant handwriting, though he couldn't avoid several mistakes. He kept asking us to write to him, "even just a line each, so that being far apart won't make us lose our affection." He was especially tortured by the possibility that we had forgotten him, "especially Lucia, who must remember that when she was little she was Papa's fiancée."

The letter from one of his fellow prisoners is dated September 9, 1945. Like the others, it's addressed to my mother, this time "accompanied by piercing pain." A month earlier, my father, transferred suddenly to a different camp, had undergone hernia surgery, "and it was there that he caught pneumonia." "There his existence ended, I cannot forget him and I dream of him always."

Papa left when I was just over three feet tall, leaving behind him only the mystery of a man I hadn't known and wouldn't have the chance to know, whom I respectfully addressed as "Sir," who didn't have time to show me what he was made of, whether he would have raised me with kicks and slaps or as a capable, tender, and affectionate confidant. Perhaps he would have called me an animal, like many of our neighbors did with their children. I was probably lucky to content myself with a doubt and a crazy mother. Indeed, in a place where my mother was a plague and an exception, despised and kept at a distance by everyone, a violent and absent father was the norm in my village. One day, perhaps, with him leaning on the balcony, bent over the railing, his stupid and vacant eyes turned outward, I would have looked at his face, bathed in sunlight, and thought that after all, I was just the daughter of an old man.

*

I haven't talked about the war because I don't know about the war. For those living deep in the countryside, down at the bottom, already poor before, and poor during and after, the war honestly wasn't a big deal. It wasn't the war that took our father from us. Papa had done it himself, leaving as a civilian to chase his dreams. My brother was just a child and wasn't called to participate in the conflict; he was a fat calf, meat for slaughter to be kept for the next time. He became a man when the games were already over, and all anyone wanted was the end. My mother and I were excluded from what was happening, once again only because we were *fimmine*.

This was the only hint that something was changing, stirring: at school, we weren't told what we needed to know; they all occupied themselves with our feelings. Fatherland, patriot, patriotic. *Fatherland* this ambiguous word, that mixes and holds together the masculine and feminine, the necessary elements at the start. A word that meant nothing to me, incapable as I was of feeling even the barest sense of community outside the home, having grown up without a father and from a hopeless feminine.

And white bread. That's all I remember. I don't even know if this bad bread was something we actually put between our teeth, mixed with white lead and plaster, equally nourishing and poisonous. Everyone said it, repeated it, that the bread was white, and I do remember it, but I'm not sure if it was really true. For me, the war remains the myth of bread mixed with dust, described with the same, dull, sparse few words that passed from mouth to mouth between the teeth of the old women of the village.

That's all the war was for us, we who had to fight the war within the bare walls of our house, with hunger, dust, and solitude. We didn't care much about the many dead our village counted; all we knew was to take care of our blood. Papa's was the only death that hit us, that changed us.

Though I wish I could say that his death brought only sadness, the truth is that its greatest legacy was stability. Finally our life proceeded at a steady pace, the work he had found far away had yielded something, and we who remained could live off the earnings. Sure, I missed him, I loved my father beyond reason, because I barely knew him and now I never would. I tried to hate him because he had abandoned us by letting himself die; we hadn't been enough for him to resist death.

Mama cried inconsolably. She made us wear black but stopped beating us for a while; Papa had had the good taste to die a hero and had unexpectedly given the three of us a reason to be proud. We were a family at last. Inevitably, my brother and I ended up seeing his death as a blessing, one we wouldn't have hoped for, in any sense of the word.

*

I remember the red of a new bicycle, a symbol of well-being. Everyone wants a bicycle at some point in their childhood. It was the same for me. I wanted everything. I should have been a devil or a man, if I desperately wanted to eat and play and have toys and talk back to adults. I wanted a bigger house and my own room, meat fish and cheese, colored pencils, a cat and a sister for company, to go swimming in the sea. I wanted my father, and sometimes I wished my mother had died instead. I wanted to go to the fair, the first prize, the bicycle. I had to participate and win. I must have been depraved if what Mama said was correct.

My father had never really been with us, but the fact that he was alive somewhere had given her the courage, the authority to order us around and scold us. With my father alive and out of the way, my mother could act as the man, with the excuse of standing in for him. When even the idea of having a father died inside us, my mother's power became paper-thin and crumbled.

My brother Giuseppe, Pino to us, often saw me as a hindrance in his grown-up affairs. But my mother was an even greater obstacle for him. *Lariceddu*[2] since birth, my brother irritated Mama at every turn. Although he wasn't handsome, all the girls liked him, and he got into a lot of trouble, seeming to think of it as his mission. My mother tried to ground him, but he'd wriggle, eel-like, out of the bedroom window. Once, to make her mad, he knocked repeatedly on the kitchen window until he was sure she was watching, then whistled loudly, as loud as he could, so that everyone would know he'd gotten away with it again. Mama obviously didn't take it well, she'd often give way to violent tears and fits of nerves, sitting alone in the kitchen on her wicker chair, her throne. If I tried intervening between the two, I'd unfailingly get a beating; Mama didn't spare me even if I was younger. I desperately wanted to be a part of those exchanges, which seemed to me full of a visceral passion that I was completely excluded from and couldn't understand. But my mother would push me away and my brother did the same. I was *nica*[3] and *fimmina*, wherever Pino went there was no place for me; he flat-out refused to bring me with him because, he said, I could make him look bad like nobody else could. Left on my own until dark, shrouded by my mother's cries as she desperately

---

2 Unattractive.

3 Small.

raised her arms to the sky calling on divine assistance, I would wait for him, my chest bursting with black restlessness.

The bicycle changed everything. There's nothing more dangerous than two enemies joining forces. I wanted to go to the fair and win first prize, my brother wanted to go to the fair for all the reasons my mother considered it a place for degenerates. We tormented her until she finally gave us permission.

It was the first time we were allowed near the tents. Every year saw the arrival of sideshow attractions, fortune-tellers, contortionists, and acrobats. There were stalls selling candy and others offering prizes for solving riddles or hitting a target. The colorful tent fabrics and flashing lights cheerfully broke up the desolate scenery of my region. Into a stretch of desert, uncultivated, probably unhealthy, and barren was gathered everything I had ever desired in my short life. A big prize raffle always took place on the last day. That year, the first prize was a red bicycle. We were allowed to go if we stayed together, so for the entire week, my brother and I left the house holding hands all the way to the fair. We let ourselves be framed by the faded window, from where my mother was surely watching.

Pino's hand would slowly loosen its grip as soon as we heard in the distance the distorted notes of a hurdy-gurdy, the popping of balloons and the festive crowd. In front of the lights of the first tent my brother would leave me and disappear until evening, when we would slowly walk home, hand in hand once again. For the whole week, I was left alone to wander around the fair, incredulous. I was happy to study objects and people so different from my everyday life that I could hardly believe they really existed. Why didn't Mama like any of this? I wished she could recognize the beauty of the fried food carts, the candy and the *pupi*[4] in their armor, buy me some, and play with me. No one had ever bought me a real toy; we were told to imagine whatever what we wanted, as long as it followed the rules set by *u parrinu*, the priest. Everything else was sewn by my mother.

The smell of fried food, baked goods, sweet and savory, but especially of sugar, warm ricotta cheese, lemon and cinnamon made

---

4 Traditional Sicilian marionettes in the guise of armored soldiers.

me suffer greatly. The bright colors decorating the almond-paste sweets pierced my eyes and stomach. Almonds. What I would have given to munch on a few, but I knew they weren't meant for me. I wasn't entitled to them. I would return home gripped by deep hunger, more of the spirit than of the guts.

On the third day, my pleading eyes convinced a little girl to come over. She was blonde, scruffy, her knees scratched from some reckless game. She wasn't a good girl; I liked her right away. She only asked me, "Sweet or salty?" and, not really knowing what to expect and sure that asking for something sweet would be too much, I said, "Salty." Half a word and *m'intisi*, she understood. The little girl moved over to a stall selling filled and fried calzones. She slid under the table like a languid cat. I saw her dirty little hand, which had been rummaging in the mud just a moment before, reach for the pastries. She grabbed one and ran toward me, making the table wobble. The stall owner noticed and started shouting . The girl reached me in a flash, took a hungry bite of her loot and then handed it to me, urging me to hurry, there wasn't time to eat the whole thing.

I don't have the words to describe exactly what I felt; it seemed to me as though I'd never really eaten before. The warm, soft dough caressed my teeth as I felt the mozzarella drip down, staining my cheeks and dress. After all these years, I can still say that that little girl, whose name I never learned, was the best friend I'd ever have. She gave me a small bite of happiness without asking for anything in return, just because she saw the need on my face. She asked nothing for herself, except the satisfaction of stealing to do me a good turn. She disappeared like she'd come, leaving me to admire, for just a few seconds, her nervous back, muscles tense around the shoulder blades twitching at every stride. I ran off too, chewing angrily, to escape the stall owner. It wasn't hard; the man was old and chased us half-heartedly, almost as if he wanted to give us time to disappear. He stopped after a few yards, cursing lazily before returning to his usual spot. That was his dose of adventure for the day, it was how the fair was; there was no fun otherwise.

I ran, looking back, terrified that our pursuer might change his mind and start chasing us. I called out to my companion in my head, seeking her support. I held the calzone tightly, feeling the orangey oil, tinted with tomato sauce, staining my fingers, unsure whether to give in to guilt or to the greedy pangs of hunger. I decided to enter one of the fair tents. Inside, no one. Just a table in the middle covered with a long dark cloth, on which stood a dirty glass ball. Two chairs, nothing else. I lifted a corner of the fabric and hid under the table to enjoy my precious loot in peace. I smacked my lips with satisfaction as I chewed, swallowing one big bite after another to stave off the moment when I'd decide it would be better to give it up and do penance. Then I heard someone entering the tent. A man and a woman. I stopped chewing right away, barely breathing to keep from making any noise. They sat down on either side of my hiding place, convinced they were alone. The fortune teller started by asking the young client what he wanted to know. I could see the tips of both their shoes, equally filthy. The boy, uncertain, asked what awaited him, if he would have a long life, what the most important events would be. I was sure he'd placed his hands in his lap; I could see the tablecloth moving, shaken by his constant fidgeting. I heard the sound of metal and imagined the woman gesticulating over the glass ball, jingling a host of cheap bracelets. I smiled at the man's naivety. The fortune teller continued for a few minutes, then grew impatient and reluctantly admitted that she couldn't see anything. She said it was as if there were two people in front of her. The boy's destiny was unclear, dual: the destiny of both a man and a woman, an adult and a child, impossible to understand. The fortune teller became annoyed, saying it had never happened to her before; I detected a hint of distress in her words. She paused for a few minutes and then resumed. Under the table, I turned toward her, carefully coordinating every fiber of my body to avoid making any noise. I was getting interested. The boy remained silent, terrified. "It's like there's someone between you and me," she admitted, disappointed. My eyes widened in surprise: she was a *real* fortune teller; she had sensed me. She said she saw a life of anger, a life of sin, a suicide, a murder, a husband, a wife. A move elsewhere, or maybe not. Blood, few friends, children, many of them and none. The fortune teller slumped back in her chair, confused. I heard the wood creaking under her weight. It was as if there were two different people in front of her, she repeated. In any case, the young man didn't seem to promise anything good. A man who doesn't walk straight, determinedly, on a sure path, is worth nothing. Annoyed, the fortune teller let slip that he would come to a bad end, that he didn't have much time left, that fate didn't want to reveal anything about him, that maybe he had done something wrong. "You will commit something terrible and lose yourself as a consequence," she said turning to us both.

Under the table, in front of the fortune teller, I thought that instead, of my family I'd be the only one to save myself, slipping through the merciless edges of the narrow gate that selected among us for our sins. My sins would slide off me, gone. I didn't want to be the one to lose myself; I wouldn't let it happen. My entire being rejected the idea that desire brings such evil; I would do everything I could to ensure that all my sins evaporated without weighing me down. The boy, on the other hand, was terribly disturbed. He jumped up before the fortune teller could finish her speech, which had taken on the tone of a curse, threw a handful of jingling coins at her and disappeared in an instant. He was surely one who lost himself; he listened to those words of guilt and accusation before he had even done anything wrong. He decided to deserve a punishment just because someone had predicted it for him.

I was lost in revolutionary thoughts when the fortune teller kicked me square in the chest. Get out of here, you leech, she yelled, pointing out that I'd received a prediction for free. I slipped out just in time to throw up everything I'd just eaten, in a double punishment. My face was clammy and sweaty, my hands trembling, my stomach empty of courage, and contorted with hunger again. I set out to find my brother so we could go home.

That evening we found Mama muttering quietly to herself. She was singing softly, occasionally breaking into quiet laughter or letting her voice rise slightly. She didn't even see us as we walked past her. I felt my throat burning, as if I were coming down with a real illness. A sore throat, a potential cough that had not yet erupted.

*

Anyway, as I was saying, the bicycle. We got up early the last day of the fair. I'd talked to my brother about the red bicycle every day on our way there. I convinced him to enter the raffle with me. If we won, we'd share the bicycle, or else he would ride it for both of us. That day he didn't let go of my hand in front of the tents; we went on together to where the raffle would take place, to win. We sat on a couple of rickety chairs among the many still available at the foot of the stage. My brother headed to the booth selling the cards with the numbers on them. He only bought one for the both of us to share. We waited almost an hour for the raffle to begin, while the crowd grew larger and the murmuring more solid. The smell of sweat, dirty teeth, confused shouts. The rough, merry crowd of a village fair gathering around us like a threat. At last, the emcee stepped forward—a small, very thin man, hunched over his own guts. He shuffled his feet as he walked, clutching a tin megaphone in one hand and a cloth bag in the other. He moved to the center of the stage, stopped, turned to the audience and waited. He waited until he deemed it right, moving his head from right to left, peering at us all. Then he raised the megaphone, took a deep breath, and started shouting. He introduced the fair, introduced himself, introduced the game and the prizes at stake. He shuffled the numbers in the cloth bag, pulled out a small token and shouted: Let's get started, 36! The crowd roared with joy, as if everyone, by some miracle, had managed to cross off 36 on their card. A group of old men began howling with delight. 41! The shouts faded out, became less frantic; luck was starting to make its selection. I felt every bone in my body become dense, alert. The moderator looked around to see if anyone was ready to claim the smallest prize, awarded for two numbers in the same row. Silence. We watched him intently. He shuffled again, pulled out a token: 74! And then again, 87! At last, someone stood up, waving their card, to claim their prize. A middle-aged man who was invited to come onto the stage. The emcee didn't even check the card; he handed the man a ricotta-filled cannolo. He waited for the first winner to return to his seat and then, eying us all suspiciously, plunged his hand into the cloth bag and began to shuffle: 45! And then, 41! Nerves taut, the crowd shouted, "*Nisciu*, already called!" Meanwhile, I was carefully rechecking our card, lending my eyes to my brother, who seemed more interested in the competitors than the numbers. He was watching something, seeing something.

The only number we'd crossed off so far was 36. The bicycle suddenly seemed out of reach. 24! We had it, I crossed the number off with a smile, lit up by a new, albeit faint, hope. 79! Again, I couldn't believe it! They weren't in the same row. A woman stood up to collect two salamis, a loaf of bread, and a caciotta cheese. But I wasn't discouraged, we had a higher goal. 23! I fantasized about the comfortable saddle, the sound of the wheels spinning at full speed. My brother would finally take me with him; I wouldn't be a disgrace anymore. 38! We had it, I crossed it off. We'd be free to move around, maybe even go all the way to the sea together. 12! Mama didn't want us to venture too far out, convinced that going a long way off was the same thing as getting lost, as betraying, as forgetting. 57! Two kids got up, quivering with excitement for their unexpected win. They'd hoped for something better, you could see it in their faces, but being among the winners was still something to brag about. 3! I crossed it off, trying to suppress my excitement: it was clear to me that otherwise we'd never win. I'd convinced myself that I could control the outcome of the raffle with my feelings. 19! I knew it, I was doing well, we had this one too, I crossed it off. 90! Mama didn't want us to go near the beach because she was afraid something bad might happen to us, like the two girls a few months back who'd been raped and killed. She told us their bodies were found half-buried in the wet sand. I had never seen the beach. 86! But from my brother's stories, it couldn't be a place where something so horrible could happen. Maybe. 55! I crossed it off. Maybe Mama had made up a story to keep us safe. Tell me all about the sea, I would always ask, and my brother would it as a mass of blue, green, and azure sheets in constant motion, crashing with beer foam onto a valley of black pebbles. 22! To tell the truth it was me who insisted he find comparisons to describe the sea. At first Pino would get annoyed and clam up. 15! When I kept insisting, he'd sigh and complain before saying it was just water, so much water. And yet I couldn't picture it: an inert expanse of water, unworkable, uninhabitable, undrinkable, ungraspable. Ineffable, in other words. A liquid expanse, that, 66!, couldn't find a place in the mind, at least not mine, always on fire. 18! So I tried to understand by leaning on Pino's thoughts and memories, which I asked him to translate into words.

39! I closed my eyes and tried to feel the pebbles under my feet and between my toes, just like he'd described them. Picturing the sea when you don't know it is a vain effort, I only realized later on when I finally saw it for myself. 39! There's nothing to understand. 6! I remembered the raffle and opened my eyes again. We had the number, I crossed it off. 27, which came shortly after, as well. Next to us, an old man with a hooked nose crossed off number 1 just a second before the emcee called it out. His ears stuck out, they were huge, alien. For an instant, I wondered if that's what had helped him detect in advance what the emcee was about to shout, reaching the words rolled up in his throat, even his thoughts and intentions. After a few seconds, I felt like an idiot. A doubt crept in: were we just pretending to play, was the game rigged? We also had number 1, I limited myself to crossing it off without saying anything, since I knew that Pino—engrossed in his silent research—wouldn't have listened. I struggled with suspicion, trying to suppress it like we did in the village with the mewling of unwanted kittens: drowning them in a bucket. 13! I crossed it off.

48! Victory is a feeling that comes alive long before it takes place. It's an idea of the senses, a premonition, when you still don't know anything. 77! We were making our way toward our goal one number at a time, shivers of pleasure coursing through us. 17! Again, one step less to take. 81! Victory doesn't just happen; it's constructed, sometimes it's faked. 30! You win when the others stop coming up with pretexts, believing themselves beaten. 14! The real gift of the winner is endurance. Luckily, it's the one thing Pino and I had never lacked and that we'd mastered and could have taught others. The one who steers a straight course is not the winner, nor the one who uses his voice, who takes advantage of the light to show off. 44!

Where I came from it was clear. Victory is a knot of knots, tied strictly and swiftly in silence, in the dark. The ends tightly secured, in the end, with your teeth. Your mouth open in a half-moon, who knows if because of the effort or in a smile.

I checked our card carefully. Among all the numbers the moderator had called out, Pino and I had collected: 36, 24, 79, 38, 3, 19, 55, 6, 27, 17, 30, 1, 44, 13. I'd checked them so many times that I can still picture them, right here, right between my eyes. There was only one square left to cross off. Our competitors must have found themselves in a similar situation, there was hardly any hope left of winning. I elbowed my brother sharply, pointing at the card. All around us, people had started clapping rhythmically, the end was near. My brother nodded.

"They don't check them," is all he whispered.

64! I was about to check, I didn't remember it. My brother leapt to his feet, snatching the paper from my hands. He started waving it like a white flag, like he was a pirate declaring unconditional surrender. In motion like this, our card looked completely filled out, as if no box was missing. Then, shouting for joy, Pino crumpled the card up, slipped it into his pocket and hugged me. We were asked to step onto the stage. I was trembling. My brother smiled and held me close, turning his head from side to side toward our opponents, giving them a reassuring look. He rubbed my shoulders and whispered tender words to me. I knew, because he'd never done so before, that it was just an act, albeit wonderfully staged. The emcee shook his hand, then bent down to my height and looked me straight in the eye. I was terrified he'd read the truth on my face. Instead, an unconvincing smile spread across his ashen features, his eyes remained glassy, lifeless, they seemed almost to give off a bad smell. He congratulated me languidly and offered me his hand, which I shook firmly. As cheaters, we had won. I finally found the courage to look my brother in the face. We were both laughing, for the first time together.

"Can you keep a secret, Luci'?" He winked at me.

"Yes." I replied, as confidently as if I were answering my teacher.

"Good girl. Me too." Pino ruffled my hair.

We smiled at each other. The bicycle now seemed to matter much less.

*

I'll never forgive myself for the week we were away and won that red bicycle. While we were gone, a man started visiting my mother, who was completely alone for the first time and incapable of saying no. She didn't tell me what happened during those visits, but from her wild reactions after each meeting, thanks to the sharp intuition of children,

I suspected, I knew what was happening. I would come home and find her praying, humming softly, or crying, and she didn't even see me. One day, a day with scattered thunderstorms, I ran into the man on our doorstep as he was closing the door behind him. He grunted in my face, almost smugly, and disappeared. From that point on, I felt that whenever I allowed myself a bit of freedom, my mother would pay the price because of the man with no language. I was tarnished with a horrendous guilt, and I couldn't do anything about it. Doubts crept into me in the shape of certainty, but I didn't want to believe the evil that was happening. I had rabid black dogs in my chest, but they couldn't tell me anything; they howled loudly. That's all. I didn't know how to face them, so I convinced myself to ignore them, hoping I was wrong. Sometimes, as children, we register things that we only understand later, allowing circumstances to write upon us truths we only intuited. When I chose to look back as an adult, I realized that I already knew, and that my father was right. The world is made of dirt and mud, at least ours is.

I've long been obsessed with my mother's pain. I suffered from it. In the endless summer of my childhood I was busy rejecting her, not acknowledging her rights nor understanding her. It took me many years, perhaps a lifetime, to see her from a different perspective. Her pain seemed to me at first incomprehensible, annoying, wounding, wrong. My mother was a dark and poisoned well; I was afraid even to get close, of shriveling up next to her. I now know that a contaminated well isn't to blame, that stagnant water has no will or defenses. It can only take in everything that others want for it. Contaminated water bears the stain of others' actions, it is violated by its tormentors and despised by everyone. I wish I could give my mother back the dignity that was taken from her. I wish I could tell the truth, her truth. I know that by telling it, I transfigure it, change its nature. I knew a person, but all I have left is a character. I paint her with patches of color, dense and harsh; I'll never know the details. This is all that remains of her.

She wasn't an affectionate mother, but I can't blame her for that. She didn't choose us, she didn't expect anything from us, while we expected everything. She may have loved my father, with a bitter, powerful love, but she hadn't been able to do the same for us. No one had taught her about love and she was never able to master her feelings. She hadn't wanted to be a mother, but it seemed that we were born solely for this purpose.

To be fair, she did try for a long time, as long as she remained lucid, to love us. She decided to celebrate my thirteenth birthday with a picnic. Papa had been away from home for seven years by then and gone from this earth for two. Mama woke me up at dawn, in high spirits. She kept shaking me, yelling that it was late and we needed to get ready. My brother had been sent for fresh eggs. Mama moved around the house like a ghost. Even then, she was shockingly thin, losing the freshness of youth day by day, she wasn't full and colorful as before. Her chest reduced to a board, she suffocated inside her usual black dress, which now hung on her like a tunic. By mid-morning, she had tied her hair back and was working tirelessly in the kitchen: she was preparing *u biancomanciari*[5] with vanilla and *cioccolatto*. The eggs were cooking in a small pot of boiling water, and the strong smell of coffee wafted through the house. Mama had bought fruits of bright colors so vivid that it seemed to me they must be fake. She'd bought bread and honey, she'd certainly spent a fortune. Our meagre two rooms had never shone so brightly. Mama was kneading almond paste, moistening it with water, softening it until it melted completely, preparing milk for us.

It appeared like magic, streaming between her tanned fingers. She was handling the metal molds, shaped like a bunch of grapes, that had belonged to her grandmother. Just like her mother before her, once the *biancomanciari* was prepared, she would place it on fragrant lemon leaves. Cooking is a dance that moves from the eyes to the hands, something you steal from others and learn by doing.

Extreme, drastic: my mother did everything as if she had to choose sides, she was a partisan. That day we were supposed to celebrate, to have fun. Me, Anna, Pino. All three of us worked tirelessly and silently to make it possible. If I remember right, we also prepared stuffed and

---

5 *Biancomangiare*, a traditional Sicilian dessert made with almond milk known for its simplicity and sweetness. Similar to blancmange, but with different ingredients.

fried eggplants and pasta with tomato sauce and basil. Pino and I weren't used to such plenty, nor could we figure out what justified such a waste of energy and money for any old birthday, for the youngest in the house. My mother was a whirlwind, we could barely keep up with her. Around noon, with everything finally ready, Anna had us pack everything into a basket, where she also placed a large, rough cloth, plates, and silverware. Then she ordered us to follow her. We set off wordlessly, to have fun. Papa would have smiled at the confident demeanor of his Annuccia, whom he had always treated, in good times and bad, as the eldest of his children.

Unable to resist his growling stomach, Pino kept reaching for the basket. Anna promptly slapped his hand away, as if she could predict his actions. We quickly crossed the arid expanse surrounding our house, until we reached fields, rows of olive trees and a hillock of crunchy grass. Mama chose a mighty tree to provide shade for our meal. With our help, she spread the cloth and set the table. She ordered us to sit. Then she smiled at us, pleased with her efforts. She looked at us desperately, not knowing how to proceed, twisting the frayed hem of her dress between her gnawed fingers. We sat there, lost in a crackling silence, none of us daring to touch anything, not even Pino. I saw my mother's gaze fix on an ant climbing determinedly onto the cloth. Then another. Anna's smile grew tense, her mood suddenly fragile. My brother lunged forward greedily, trying to grab the best portion of everything. I began to whine, my voice wavering, complaining about his bossiness. We started slapping each other and then pulling each other's hair. It was a game, maybe we didn't really know how to handle such plenty. My brother insisted on serving everyone, while I called out for Mama, swelling with frustration. Everyone knows that *a cu sparte, a megghiu parte*, the person serving gets the lion's share. I demanded justice but got a storm instead. My mother was flushed, visibly restrained, intolerant. She cried out so loudly the sky seemed to crack open. Ants spread like wildfire over the makeshift tablecloth, on our food. Their swarming presence tainted the happiness that had seemed so necessary, so important just moments before. I felt as if I had been made wrong, and I thought to myself: this is why. Anna stood up, still shouting fierce words, and headed back home, leaving us alone to watch the insects devour everything.

As a child, I often longed for a cool summer, a carefree age.

*

No matter how well they describe it to you, the sea is never what others say it is. Even today, I believe that having encountered it as an adult was a stroke of luck: I longed for it so intensely that I can still clearly recall what it means to see it for the first time. Hearing it roar is terrifying; I still find it hard to believe it's not alive. Pino shoved me violently toward the expanse of water, urging me to hurry. He was eager to take me but didn't want to admit his excitement. Girl stuff, disgusting. It was too much for me; I couldn't go in the water. Pino ran awkwardly to the foam on the shore and threw himself into the waves as if he wanted to lose himself in them. I started to shout, thinking he'd abandoned me. When he resurfaced, he was laughing wickedly, mocking me, calling me *scecca* and *bestia*, a stupid beast.[6]

From then on, we returned many times, with me sitting on the handlebars and him riding the red bicycle. Pino was becoming fond of me, he'd learned that I could be a wiseass con artist just like him. He made me his friend, teaching me about mischief. We killed lizards in the all-consuming heat, stopping along path edges as we headed toward the salty expanse. We'd stop to examine with scientific interest the hedges with their dry leaves. Pino showed me how to snatch insects and small animals with quick, guilty movements. Children's hands are perfect for taking care of certain matters, their hearts proud and sure a war machine sparing nothing. Once captured, the unfortunate creatures met a miserable end in the dusty earth and on the sides of a rock that we'd drop on them from above like a divine judgment. Pino taught me to shout while doing it. Our bicycle rides to the sea took the form of desperate pilgrimages, marked by ritual sacrifices and cries of exertion. We felt like true warriors, comrades. Those were days of burning love. I would have liked to have been a man so Pino would

---

6   *Scecca* and *bestia* mean donkey and beast, animal. Figuratively: stupid.

love me even more, to be a real companion to him, to be even with him. Still, I was content, because he wouldn't let anyone else go where I was venturing. With other women he wound up rolling around on the grass and in the bushes, but he always said none of them were right, and he kept on looking for something else.

Little by little I became more comfortable with the water. I began by no longer screaming every time my brother dove in. I'd sit at a safe distance on the sand and burying my feet in it. I would rest my chin on my knees, I closed myself up imagining I was a shell while Pino splashed around and screamed like a madman, I'd close my eyes and listen. Then I started getting closer, dipping a toe into the water. I'd pull back immediately, sit down, and think. Pino would yell and splash water at me. My body got to know the sea an inch at a time, like a chaste lover: it touched me bit by bit, encounter after encounter, the top of my foot, my ankles, my cool calves and tense thighs, my narrow hips, my goosebumps, every vertebra and rib, my timid breasts, my protruding chest bones, my proud shoulders, my long neck, my black hair, my dark eyes. In the end, it swallowed my sobs and last breath, the one just before going under. It got to know me better than anyone else, in the presence of my brother, completely unaware.

*

I like being self-possessed. Pino, my Pino, was the exact opposite; he found losing himself to be really helpful. He smoked a lot, constantly, exhaling incredibly thick smoke. He spat out billowing rings, creating a column of smoke between his nose and lips. A snake-charmer's smile crossed his face. He called me his "little beast." Pino had gnarled hands and wrinkles around his eyes, from the beginning . He offered me my first cigarette one afternoon, under a sullen sky. I fell face-first into the dirt, where the sand was still just dust among the stones. Pino pulled out every splinter, applied pressure to stop the bleeding and sucked on the wound to disinfect it. We smoked together, and I felt the veins in my face throbbing with excitement.

Pino had a way of making my knees quiver. In the evenings, after the sea, if he'd caught anything, he'd eviscerate it, pulling the guts out from the head. I felt just like those fish, torn apart from the skull and stripped of my backbone. I couldn't afford to disappoint him; I'd fulfill any request so he wouldn't think I was insufficient.

One day, he handed me a pair of scissors, asking me to cut his hair. I accepted, terrified of leaving him disfigured. I worked with surgical precision for over an hour, without speaking. The result was unexpectedly pleasing, we both agreed as he combed his hair and admired his reflection. I was proud of myself, feeling my heart in my ears and the blood rising to my cheeks. That night, I dreamed of descending a million stairs, clutching a comb and a gleaming pair of scissors in my fist. The darkness seemed close, but it never arrived.

We often walked together, quietly. I stayed a little behind him, while Pino walked the bicycle lazily. I dangled my arms in the tall grass, gathering the wild oat seeds to finger and then plucked them while asking silly questions. How many children will you have?, I'd ask before tossing them at his back. It was how kids made predictions. Not a single seed ever stuck to him. Neither of us was meant to give life; it was hard to believe we ourselves had ever been created. We were enough for each other, we'd always been there for each other.

I remember one night. Lying next to each other in the bare room, our faces close to each other, we closed our eyes to sleep. I was restless as usual, unable to fall asleep. I was afraid of wasting our time together, that when we woke up, Pino wouldn't want me with him anymore. He could feel me tossing and turning in bed. Give me your hand, Luci', he whispered, pretending to be slightly annoyed. I squeezed his hand in mine. Sleep, Luci', is all he said, as if it were a magic spell he was reciting from the edge of sleep. My brother fell asleep in an instant. In his rhythmic breathing, I heard the sound of our sea. For a moment, I was happy. And it worked, I was asleep within seconds.

*

Our false winning of the red bicycle sparked a brief period of comradeship, it made us recognize each other as siblings and deluded us into thinking that we'd be together forever, from then on. I sometimes find myself thinking that only with Pino was I truly alive, which would mean my life lasted just two years. Two pleasant, aimless years, like the moment when you touch your belly and then between your legs under the scorching sun, to enjoy the warmth of the skin and the touch of your hand at the same time. Two years spent close together after years of indifference, too many spent in the anguish of separation.

But my brother received extreme unction on the verge of adulthood, the same day I got my first period. Of the two, I'd been warned that it would happen. Mama had told me that a bleeding wound would open up and it would only heal when I was no longer of any use. Every month, I would be reminded of how dirty we are, of our sins. We both bled, me for the first time, him for the last. Coughing, he spat out so much blood it seemed as if his lungs had dissolved into a red river. He had wanted so badly to grow up, chasing the finish line by biting onto time, grabbing what he could, only to be left clutching air in his stiff, cold fists without ever having the chance to become a man. The shock of these events broke the last shred of my mother's intellect and ended my childhood.

It was actually the second time my brother had faced eternal darkness. The first time was during the epidemic. The fever that had already killed lots of people had confined him to bed for days, turning his eyes and skin yellow. My mother decided to face the situation by making a vow, she promised she would no longer touch coffee if the Lord granted her the favor of saving her son. Normally, Anna would let streams of black coffee, with absolutely no sugar, spill onto the saucer to cool before sipping it, holding back the greedy urge to gulp it down. Despite her efforts to hide it, we could all see the pleasure it gave her. No matter how hard she tried, she never convinced anyone that she was content with her life. We knew that small indulgences like coffee, or a cigarette secretly rolled and smoked on a special day, kept her going. At first, her sacrifice seemed useless, my brother continued to lose color and strength. We despaired of being able to save him, the Lord was deaf and wanted him only for Himself. The epidemic was a silent, fierce animal, a predator from within. My mother cried all her tears when the priest left.

The next day, wrapped like an ancient nobleman in the sheet that had nearly heard him breathe his last, my brother rose up rigidly in the middle of the bedroom. He'd chosen to survive. Unable to contain her enthusiasm, Mama grabbed a wooden spoon from the old, scratched table and slammed it on his shoulder, shouting that he'd given her a huge *scantu*[7] with no reason, as usual.

When Pino got sick the second time, no one in the family really worried; we were sure he'd found a way to outsmart even death. My mother seemed almost amused at first. Pino himself didn't seem to accept the possibility of leaving so soon; he wanted to be an aviator, to go on lots of missions, and become a war hero. He told me that he was certain he would crash, maybe in some remote corner of the desert, just like Papa had. The local peoples would rescue him and heal him with their magic potions. He was sure that once he returned home, he'd find a wife among the ranks of Red Cross nurses caring for the veterans. She'd be beautiful, of course, and willing to marry him despite his infamous unattractiveness. Pino was sure he'd find a wife from the North, who would truly save and heal him, taking him far away. He talked about the daughters he'd have, he wanted two, he'd already picked out their names. Slapping his forehead and laughing, he said he was the type to only have *fimmine*, a man shooting blanks. He pictured a long, wonderful, and full life, ending peacefully of old age when the time was right.

Sometimes I think that if he had survived, he might have had to give up flying for one of those ridiculous twists of fate, an joke like flat feet or short-sightedness.

He seemed invincible, he was not, his end didn't come when the time was right. Anna sprang into action and quit smoking. The previous time, she'd dragged him back by his hair from the cauldron of dead souls with her sacrifices and prayers. Not this time. Under our astonished gazes, he too was forced to succumb.

My brother's name was Giuseppe, Pino to me, and now I struggle to remember even the outlines of his face. His loss caused unbearable pain, he was my greatest love. My head, my head, my head. My head was bursting with pain. Pain that rose from my nostrils to my left temple, poisoning half of my face like an infected root. The open hand

---

7   Scare.

of a monster, squeezing mercilessly on part of my face.

What would become of my memory if I didn't keep the few photographs that recall everything about my life? Perhaps it's only thanks to them that Pino and everyone else appear to me in dreams, when I know what they are thinking as if I were thinking it myself. There's a black-and-white postcard that captures us as raw youths in our days of friendship, his last days, dressed in our best clothes, sitting close together on the curved edge of a white marble fountain. Pino is hugging me with his right arm, his hand gently surrounding my shoulder. I'm resting my left elbow on his lanky thigh. My black dress, with three-quarter-length sleeves and the hem well below the knee, can't dampen my happy aura, the sparkle of my sharp white smile, my full and firm calves. Pino, his neck constricted by a tie with diagonal stripes, his wrist encircled by a classy watch I don't remember and can't explain, moved his head as the photographer snapped the picture. His face is a cloud of smoke and uncertain thoughts, unsure and troubled.

The night he died, I didn't dream of Pino; I dreamed of my mother: I was walking down a long country lane, a tree-lined path. I finally found myself in front of an old, abandoned farmhouse, built with stones and rocks. Anna, engulfed in an exquisite white nightgown, almost like a wedding dress, stood on the top-floor terrace, looking down without blinking. She didn't notice me; she let herself fall, without putting up resistance, as if she were made of nothing. Pierced by deep sorrow, I turned to walk back slowly. I didn't need to worry about the fall; it wouldn't have caused any harm: I knew that standing on that balcony, Anna was already dead.

*

Mama lost herself, completely. Once the men of the house were gone, there was no longer any reason to stay.

I had an aunt left, my father's sister, sometimes she'd come to look after us. Taking pity on us, she decided to stay over for a few days, in order to decide what should be done. Otherwise, she was sure that my mother would have given in to the temptation of fading away, permanently and deliberately. She sent me up North, to find a job. I was done with school, my father and brother had abandoned us. Without our men, almost with no resources, our situation was heading toward the worst.

My aunt was a witch, a fortune teller, renowned in the village, she sold readings in exchange for milk, bread and eggs, sometimes even a chicken if things were going well. Like my father, she had chosen a life that was a flickering flame. My mother had never gotten along with her, but by then Anna was just a semblance of herself, good-looking but with no substance, a well-woven wicker basket with nothing inside. Irretrievably foolish, in a constant stupor, her senses no longer spoke to her. She smiled happily at her sister-in-law, probably seeing in her only a sign of the past, a link to happier times.

When my mother completely lost her mind, my aunt decided to save me. She placed her hands on my temples, both hers and mine continuously sweating, and said, looking at me alarmed, that a house with a madwoman and a fortune teller was already as full as a hard-boiled egg.

"*Non c'è rui senza tri, pigghia u trenu.*"[8]

Smiling, she added that I wouldn't struggle to find a husband, I was as beautiful as my mother and a witch like her and Papa. As for her, she would make sure that Mama lacked nothing. Anna would always have company, perhaps more food than she had ever allowed herself and that now she would eat more readily. The eyes before which she wanted to appear right and suitable were no longer there. I was happy with the proposal; it gave me some independence and provided my mother with the necessary care.

My aunt chose my life for me, in return asking only that I send her some money each month once I'd found a job and settled down. I left enveloped in warmth, filled with warmth, from the insides of my mouth on down, further. Like my father.

I spent the whole journey carefully selecting the childhood memories I would throw out the window. The trip seemed endless, as if the train had no real destination. For part of the journey, we were loaded onto a ship and crossed a stretch of water. I wondered if

---

8   "(Bad) things always come in threes, take the train."

I was going to visit my brother. Exhausted, I fell asleep. I dreamed of a gray horse, stained with gunpowder, alone on a smoking battlefield. Among hundreds of dead bodies, it wandered tiredly, almost white in the sunlight that barely penetrated through a layer of clouds. To me, its solitude, in the midst of a deathly carpet, was the saddest, most unjust thing.

When I opened my eyes again, my head was throbbing painfully on the left side. The other passengers moved slowly, they seemed to me as if made of sand. Outside, the streets gradually turned white with snow, another thing I'd never seen. Leaving home, moving up the continent, tasted like salt. I thought about the person driving the train, a monster with furious, glowing eyes. I imagined them close by, man or woman, a human being like me, perhaps with the same thoughts and similar feelings. Both of us were traveling, alone, into the darkness of the night.

FALL

It happens sometimes our bodies don't speak to us. I found myself, without remembering how, on the gray platform of the arrival station, so different from the dusty red departure station. My eyes were fixed ahead, veiled, as if looking at the future that awaited me. I see myself from the outside, the handle of a cardboard suitcase clenched in my right hand, blocking others from disembarking. Motionless and numb, as if confronted by a cage of frenzied beasts, petrified by the fear of being torn apart. My mind was still filled with the endless dry fields, the pale stone walls, the red and white chairs outside the houses of the old folks, the expanses of farms that separated me from the village. The strange feeling that I had been awakened the morning after being hanged. Looking back felt impossible and painful, almost as if I were convinced that the train had erased everything as it sped along. I'd ended up in a completely different land, with hard and frozen air that filled my insides painfully. I no longer sweated; I was prey to other kinds of fluids, starting with a trickle of mucus that slid out of my nose. I made my way with difficulty out of the entrance, prompted by the complaints and insults the other passengers aimed at me. Weighed down by the journey, I stood in the rain, trembling with cold. The frost, a monster I'd never met before, bit at my ankles and ungloved fingers, threatening to take them away. Emptiness gnawed at my stomach. I was no longer in my dusty southern village. I was new in a way that no one wants to be, inexperienced, incapable.

Catena, a woman from our village who was now over fifty, was waiting for me at the station, wilting under the shelter of a dark umbrella. My aunt had slipped a letter into my pocket to show to her as soon as I arrived, to remind her of the expected gratitude for a favor she owed my aunt. Catena would take me in, at least until I got settled. Sometime ago, my aunt had broken an egg over Catena's head, whispering dark words with obscene sounds, when Catena had despaired of finding a husband and had already grown accustomed to the plain, black clothes of mourning or of solitude, to unkempt hair, to a life of no value. Exactly one year later, a husband had finally arrived, a husband from the North, no less, which was certainly worth double. On my part, I wasn't sure my aunt could really be credited with the responsibility and honor of the marriage. Nevertheless, the village gossiped about the matter for a long time. Catena, who had never been beautiful, had now become irreversibly soft: how could she be desirable to a civilized, respectable man, moderately well-off, and what's more who came from the continent? This is why people said my aunt was a miracle-worker and that there must have been something strange about him. Having shared life there for a while, I can say we're talking about a man of scandalous banality, silent and too lazy to be genuinely good-hearted. A man whose mission in life was simply to be, to remain, and then disappear.

But Catena wasn't interested in love; she'd never even thought about it. What she needed was an opportunity, something she had long prayed for, a way to escape and to enjoy a life of ease envied by all the village women who were left, and they were, to eat the dust. She wasn't particularly wealthy, but she could afford a maid to handle morning chores and a real private bathroom in the house, absurdly tiled in white and always immaculate, as if it were a place of worship rather than for unleashing the intestines. It was already much more than I'd hoped for and was used to. I was empty, smooth as the dry stone of my village, and everything suited me fine.

Looking at Catena, one felt a certain pity in the heart, and also annoyance, like the slow, agonizing path of fingernails on a chalkboard. It was clear that she made a dramatic attempt to look beautiful and elegant, to reach the level required by the new life that fate had allowed her, by the position and milieu in which she was surrounded. As time passed, I realized that Catena, in a way that I had never allowed myself to do, not even at first, must have filled her head with expectations that kept her from seeing her real condition and the meager results of her efforts. As much effort as she put into studiously performing her part, elegance slipped through her fingers no matter what she did. She was a coarse peasant woman, wrapped in clothes that never seemed to fit a body that had worked long and hard; it was almost as if she'd stolen her entire wardrobe. To make matters worse, she had an absolute lack of taste. Never made up, she relied entirely on her hairstyles, on which she spent a great deal of time and money, boasting a large collection of wigs. On special occasions, she'd apply a hint of rouge to her cheeks.

Catena was as dry as I was when I met her, but somehow, the time we spent together helped us find our own private balance. She had never had children, and I could barely count on myself; I was young and unsure of myself and still had no idea who I was ... if any of us ever is permitted to know it. Each in our own loneliness, we kept each other company.

*

First of all, she helped me find a job. Right away, she recommended me to a friend of hers as a maid suitable for all household chores. She explained that I had strong hands and was accustomed to hard work, that I didn't speak out of turn and knew how to be useful, despite not being a complete peasant, since I had completed mandatory education fairly well. She lied, saying I had never stolen and that I was trustworthy, although she herself knew the pinch that grips anyone who has had nothing in life when faced with abundance.

Without my realizing it, time, which had started off disoriented, turned into weeks and then months. I also began to look after two children, the offspring of another wealthy woman whom Catena had started to associate with after her marriage, pretending to be friends. With both jobs, I had the impression that Catena had mentioned my name more for herself than to provide me with work, or at least that her interest in the matter was equal to mine, albeit not of an economic nature. Catena wanted me among those people's rooms so I could personally gather information to report back to her. A tired vendetta against those who still asked her, as they later asked me, if it was true that we enjoyed growing tomatoes in the bathtub and letting chickens roam the living room.

My house was little more than an empty cardboard box; these people, on the other hand, filled their homes with objects that had no practical use, almost as if our hands shouldn't have to do anything. What struck me the most was the superfluous, the constant, invasive presence of knick-knacks that served no purpose. Catena, on her part, perversely enjoyed tormenting herself over the difference between her condition and that of these women. Even though she'd earned herself a husband and a respectable home, she could never reach, match, or surpass them as she dreamed of doing. She was still a wild creature just like me, ready to stealthily slip a pretty trinket into her pocket just for the simple pleasure of touching and owning something luxurious. She forced me to tell her long evening stories, listening tensely like a hyena on the hunt, while the uneven snoring of her husband echoed from the master bedroom.

"What do children smell like?" she asked.

But at first I didn't know how to answer her. Then she became insistent, demanding an effort from me. I closed my eyes and tried to recall the sweet, almost nauseating smell of the fragile little beings entrusted to me.

"Like what we don't have," I finally replied, disappointing her. Strangely, for me, I had no words to explain it.

Then she would beg me to describe the silverware, ceramics, curtains and carpets, lace and starched linens and jewels, to which I had partial access only if the ladies forgot them on their nightstands after taking them off before bed. I imagined them massaging their sore, red earlobes, worn out by the weight of pearls. For Catena's sake, I opened closets, touched fabrics, brought them to my nose, tried on shoes, immediately feeling the shape of someone else's foot. I counted hats, scarves, bags, and of course I was asked to pay particular attention to wigs and toupees. Drunk on details, Catena listened to me in silence, slumped in her chair until she eventually smiled. She felt satisfied then, as after a hearty dinner and went to bed, leaving me alone prey to a spinning head.

Catena would never have a child, so I occupied the nursery. Sometimes, unable to sleep, I'd lie motionless in the small bed, staring fixedly in one direction. I memorized the room and its furnishings, which were simple and modest. Yet it still didn't seem enough; something didn't quite add up, and I kept my eyes glued to a corner, a piece of furniture, a hand-embroidered quilt. It felt like I was slowly sinking into a sea of details, even though there weren't any.

The glaring white of the walls made the light filtering through the room's only window to my left bounce onto the wall opposite the bed. The pure white curtains couldn't even hold back the moonlight, and they often swayed and danced, even with the windows closed. Beneath the windowsill, there was a wicker chest covered in pillows embroidered with the same pattern as the quilt. Raising my head, much to my dismay, I could see the dirty feet of Christ on a crucifix made of dark wood, over which Catena had placed an olive branch to ward off ill luck. Catena didn't seem very religious, but she'd never admit otherwise. Religion was simply part of her upbringing and her past, like all of us; she wouldn't dream of questioning it any more than she would have questioned grammar or mathematics.

Facing the bed, on the opposite wall, hung a portrait of a man with an unreadable expression on his face. The first few nights I spent in that room, it kept me from sleeping. One day, I got up the courage to ask Catena who he was. You don't know him, she answered, but I already knew that, and so the conversation ended there. I was forced to get used to the painting, until I no longer noticed it. A nightstand, an oval rug in the middle of the room, a small wardrobe for my few belongings, and nothing more. The wooden floor creaked with every slight movement, often forcing me, if it disturbed the night's silence, to bend my back and twist my mouth to the side, revealing my teeth.

When sleep refused to come until morning, I would turn on the light and jot down the parts of my accounts that Catena had liked the most.

*

First of all, I needed a dress; I couldn't show up at someone else's house that way, our way. Catena took me to buy one, and we chose a dark green one. Cinched at the waist with a fabric belt, it wrapped around my hips and was decorated with small white flowers. From the hem and the three-quarter-length sleeves much of me protruded, bare, outside. For the first time, I wore something that caught the eye; I felt like a giant, too tall, too imposing, too much. Who did I think I was? I hunched my shoulders as I looked at myself in the mirror, dark curls piled messily in front of my face. Standing next to me, with a look of serious approval, Catena placed the palm of her open hand between my shoulder blades.

"*Dritta hai a stari,*" she said.

Straight. And so I straightened my back.

*

I'd get up at dawn, even if I hadn't slept a wink, tidy up my room, and wait seated on the bed for Catena to join me. I'd let my legs wiggle nervously, pick at my nails until they were sore; her arrival always seemed to be postponed by a few more seconds, leaving me waiting forever. We'd all have breakfast together and then I would leave, just as the maid rang the apartment doorbell.

I'd take a rattling tram, white and yellow. It was one of my first discoveries after moving. I enjoyed the crescendo of squeaks that came with its acceleration, making conversation impossible, the sudden braking that violently rocked the passengers. It battled against all of us, it said be quiet, it said fall down. I liked looking out the window, wiping it with my sleeve after breathing a warm cloud onto its surface directly from my restless insides. I'd lift my elbow and quickly draw frantic circles with the fabric of my coat. I'd look back outside and everything would appear clearer and sharper; I was so satisfied with my work, almost as if, instead of cleaning the glass, I'd managed to wash the street.

The street however was always smooth, clean, dark asphalt. No dust or cats, no uncertainty wandering about, they were either resolved or lost forever, to die from warm dampness and then from cold dampness. Crushing loneliness weighed on my shoes and in the depths of my pockets, slowing my steps until I reached the threshold of the apartment where I was to work that day. Every day. I was in a city of grays and pink, of arcades and rain. For us, rain is an unexpected blessing that comes rarely but with a dark violence, breaking the midafternoon mugginess just long enough for you to seek a shelter that soon becomes useless. There in the city it was a persecution that lasted days on end, nullifying the passage of time, filling the squares with a milky, infirm light. It seemed to me like a sick city, or like a city that made me sick, which is the same thing.

So it was with infected thoughts that, once, I wandered through the usual colorful rugs and shiny floors of the lady whose house I managed. Kneeling with my feet planted on the ground and the rest of my body leaning forward, I was waxing the floor, almost at the end of my workday, my back broken and my apron damp. Out of the corner of my eye, I noticed a flicker that unsettled me. I stopped and sat down cautiously. Again, something was moving, the same warm color as the wood beneath me. Horror and disgust cut through my chest: a long, brittle insect ran swiftly and disjointedly, its intentions unclear, sometimes fluttering its wings with an infernal hiss. It finally decided to stop, threateningly still. In an instant, the room closed in on me, pushing me toward the horrible beast, which wielded a disturbing power given its size. It seemed to carry with it the very essence of raw life, and it terrified me. I was powerless against it; it won its war. It stared at me, intent on annihilating me, secure in its power.

I don't know if seconds, minutes, or even hours passed. I stared at the insect and it stared back, much braver than me. It reveled in its fetid presence, even more incongruous amid such lavish wealth, and it liked it, which seemed even more unbelievable to me. Even wealthy ladies share rooms with cockroaches. Maybe they never notice them, because people like me are tasked with killing them before it comes to that. I shouldn't have felt what I felt; I should have acted with blunt determination and slapped it away with an open hand. But I couldn't; I felt dizzy, afraid of throwing up. I spared the insect out of ineptitude and fear, not pity. I felt severed from the earth, I didn't know which way to go.

I had the sudden desire to witness some tragedy in that polished house, so I could tear my hair out, feigning inconsolable despair.

Sharing in someone else's tragedy, without truly understanding it, brings the strange pleasure of feeling involved, of being important. Sinking into abjection, into deep misery, can be enjoyable. I told myself that without disaster we'd have nothing to discuss.

A dark energy returned to me suddenly; I found within me the competence I'd always admired in our tough women, who carry tragedy and know how to solve it. I thought again of the insect, this time without fear. I killed it, feeling sympathy for it.

I had completed my tasks, including the last, unexpected one, and so I left, weighed down by a strange feeling. Even though I hadn't planned to in advance, I took a different route home. It was raining and I didn't have an umbrella, but I avoided the arcades anyway; I didn't want to meet anyone, as if I had ill intentions and the need to carry them out in the shadows. I followed with my gaze the fringed edge of the snow-covered mountains, having a random walk, as if lost in an overflowing basin, drawn down by a centripetal force toward the drain hole. Clarity and awareness sometimes interrupted by banks of fog so bright they erased everything, an unexpected relief for which I didn't even pray. I was used to the torment of my constant presence, so awkward that it deprived me of sleep and pressed painfully on my forehead, such that I could never ignore the knots, which constantly demanded to be resolved.

There was suddenly a sign, appearing out of nowhere, who knows how far from home. On it was written "Creamery," and I had no idea what that meant. It had to do undoubtedly with food, with sweets, as the sugary smell of milk in the air suggested, but the shop was so fancy that I almost believed I was in front of a jewelry store. Whatever these creams were, they must have been special. It was now raining half-heartedly, and a clingy wind was blowing and getting stuck in the fog. In front of the windows a row of light wooden chairs had been placed, all empty. I leaned forward, going past them with my torso and bringing my rigid hand to my forehead, shielding my eyes in an attempt to gather more information. I didn't see anything. I went in. There was no one behind the counter. I glanced around; the furnishings, a bare minimum, were of a glacial white. On the right, displayed prominently, two large containers held hot beverages, constantly stirred by a plastic paddle swirling round and round. Soft waves formed, surfacing and piercing the liquid. The labels read *"zabaione"* and "chocolate." Laid out in neat rows, bags sealed with gold ribbons and filled with colored pralines, meringues, and chocolate-covered candied fruit tormented my eyes.

There they were, behind the glass counter: the creams, arranged in a stretch of silver baskets. Atop each lid, a sphere sparkled, refracting light in all directions. As before when I was a child at the fair, I thought that pastries are one of the few excesses worth cultivating.

Turning around again, I caught sight of a huge mirror on the left. I saw my reflection, mouth open and moist, eyes bright, cheeks flushed. The expression of one still feeling pleased at having succeeded in killing. It was as if I'd recognized someone in that face, in my face, for the first time. From behind, I heard a whistle. I started to call out but suddenly was overcome by nausea. A void formed in my heart, my knees almost gave way. For a moment my strength left me. Overwhelmed by a magical terror, I ran outside, letting the door slam behind me. For the second time in my life, a craving linked with a premonition and a prediction.

My mother died that day, and I had felt it coming.

*

Her broken life broke something inside me, too. I fell ill. I stayed confined to bed, struggling to get up, unable to speak. As it is only seldom that I can say of my life "I don't remember," my thoughts unraveled and so retain of this period little more than nothing, which if it is hard to hear it is almost impossible to convey in words.

I hadn't seen my mother in a year, and I'd never see her again, exactly as I had hoped and feared on the day I left her. I desperately wanted to bring her to me, into my room; my whole life was concentrated in one point, in the effort to fulfill myself and reconcile her with existence. Instead, I only saw her when I involuntarily let loose my grip. I seemed to glimpse her with the vividness of a concrete presence. I dreamed with wide, vacant eyes, motionless in bed.

The same as when I entered, with slow steps, our kitchen while she was with her back to me. Mama sat on her wicker throne, busy peeling tangerines. Her hair was gathered in a tidy, delicate gray bun. Her dim gaze lingered on those precious peels, tearing them into pieces as they slipped off the knife tip. She always did this; after meals, her plate was full of orange rinds, fit for the hens. Outside, beyond the windowsill, darkness filled an inkwell to the brim, without a single star, much like my heart.

Or else I happened to admire her enjoying fresh fish with gusto, as only we know how to do. She gripped the head with greasy fingers and pulled off the savory cheeks, scooped out the eyes and chewed on them with delight. Finally, she slurped noisily on the brain, almost drinking it: the prize morsel. I hadn't eaten fish since I moved to the North; I wouldn't eat it that way in public anymore. Mama never saw me, she couldn't. In fantasies, you look inward; no fantasy ever takes note of you.

One evening she was sitting on the bench under the window. Dressed all in black, she looked almost painted against the backdrop of my bright room, absurd as a punch in the eye. Threads of yellow light intertwined on her cheeks as she tried to sit neatly, waiting. She turned her head this way and that, anxiously. She moved to open her mouth but stopped herself and said nothing. She was decidedly younger than when I had known her; uneasy, yes, but without a whirlwind in her head. I wanted to speak with her, to see her move, so intensely that I woke up. It was the middle of the night, and I was inconsolably alone.

I had been a smart child, but sometimes being smart can be a disadvantage. From a young age, you get used to understanding so many things that you start to believe that nothing can get past you, so you overlook the details. Intent on the sophisticated understanding of everything else, we leave aside what's closest. I wondered if I'd ever understood her. We had been distant all our life together, I had rejected her in my desperate attempt to keep Papa close. Mama was the crazy mother, a burden, the natural outcome of a troubled family history of madness and suicides. I hadn't been able, I hadn't wanted, to see the worst hidden by my father, but she'd been enough. I thought then that if they were like a beautiful fresh apple, red and shiny, my father was the half I'd always wanted and knew how to accept, the juicy and inviting one that I'd devour in just two bites; the other half, the bruised one, ready for worms, was my mother. My crazy mother. Whom I always carry behind, within me, whom I inevitably resemble in some way. My father had the easy task of fulfilling a comfortable position. I would have loved him anyway even if he hadn't deserved it in any way. In those days, hungrier than usual, I took the first bite of the second half too, I recognized my mother and started truly to know myself.

Catena was very worried. She didn't know about my visions; I decided not to tell her so as not to scare her. She would undoubtedly have tried to find a way to make them stop. She brought me hot broth and encouraged me to swallow it, nodding as I did. *Ajava*, she said, *mancia*. Come on, eat. It's a sin not to. Then, exhausted, she noticed that I'd become too thin, that my breasts had disappeared, that I had almost no curves left. After a month, even my period stopped.

"*Figghia mia, vuoi trasere 'n un coddu ri buttigghia?*"[9] she'd despair. But I couldn't answer her; guilt closed my throat up.

A letter arrived from my aunt: she extended her greetings and condolences, she was thinking of me, she prayed for Anna and for us, and apologized for not being able to do more. Magic doesn't reach that far, she explained. She described every detail of the funeral, occasionally dwelling so deeply in the futile and dramatic pleasure of writing that it was easy to imagine oneself there again, in mourning, holding a beautiful red flower. The cemetery of rough and porous stone, Mama's grave under an ancient tree, weighed down by its weeping foliage.

My aunt didn't leave out a single detail and lingered on a disturbing aspect; she regretted having to report it to us but believed it was such an ominous sign that it had to be told. Here's what happened: as my mother's coffin was being carefully lowered into the ground, the rope holding it snapped, causing the coffin to abruptly fall sideways. Several people tried to remedy the situation, to straighten it out, but for a whole hour, there wasn't much they could do. The priest exploded into a rage and repeatedly crossed himself, clear proof that much of our superstition survived deep inside us all, and therefore in him as well.

---

9 "My child, do you want to cap a bottle of wine?" .

Men competed to find a solution, as if to verify their worth in terms of intelligence and prowess. The women exasperatedly chanted the usual laments, which by then had become an unbearable persecution. My aunt wrote also that one of them actually was just moving her mouth, having gotten too tired of emitting any sound.

I think everyone has experienced it, when a moment of sadness and intense stress dissolves into hearty laughter. I wasn't sure how much more I could suffer and endure, so I started laughing. Catena and I couldn't help it. We laughed until our stomachs hurt, tears welling up. Mine turned into crying in an instant, and I melted like wax, releasing the pain with joy.

*

One of the things that poor people also lack is time. It didn't matter that I was no longer capable of living or walking; I had to return to work, and despite having grown fond of me, Catena started urging me to resume my duties with the ladies.

The hours spent with the children were a special punishment. They didn't spare me any curiosity, torturing me with sharp questions about my mother's death and cruel remarks about my thinness. They observed with a certain pleasure that their mother had explained to them that I was an orphan and that they should be kind to me. I tried to be alert and attentive, perhaps as a form of protection against the absurd feeling that they didn't exist. A kind of protection, maybe.

The house was filled with bulky paintings, somber in color and subject. Over time I'd gotten in the habit of telling the children stories describing these images whose original meaning I didn't know. I succeeded pretty well at entertaining them with words, easier than using dolls or playing make-believe. I was completely unable to pretend I was someone else; it seemed wrong to me, even as a game. The mind works in curious ways: for that whole period, I'd never really noticed one of the larger paintings, though I walked by it several times a day, for hours at a time, and so had never told the children its story. They were the ones who showed it to me, dragging me in front of the imposing canvas. Tell us what it means, they ordered. I focused my gaze on it, and they respected my silence, well aware that that's where stories came from. Despite their youth, they were already comfortable with the fact that my time depended on their wishes. My part of satisfaction lay in managing, at least for a while, to control the will to which I would later have to submit. We'd play a game of cat and mouse, not always sure who was chasing and who was running away.

Three women with pale white skin stood in a row against a backdrop of trees and woods, with a winged child and a plump pheasant at their feet. On the right, a young man draped in rich fabric was lying on a rock. Starting from the left, the first woman, in profile, was looking at him keenly. An exquisite crown adorned her curly blonde tresses. The second one, in the center, was looking at me. She wore a helmet and was dressed in red. She was undoubtedly my favorite. The last one, enveloped in a blue cloth, was almost entirely exposed, showing her breast, with her hair falling loose on her shoulders. Her ears sparkled with crystal stones. I couldn't inspect her face; her eyes were downcast. The man was tiredly offering her a golden apple.

I pointed at him. He likes her best, I told the children, a bit incredulous. Of course, said the little boy. His sister added, knowingly, that it was because she was the most beautiful.

"I don't understand this story," I said, annoyed, refusing for the first time to serve my young masters. I felt tired. If you want, you tell the story, I added, not knowing which of the two I was addressing. The children started talking. I closed my eyes and stopped listening.

*

In my private goings-on, Anna's death was a sudden deafness. Objects seemed to have a life of their own and felt foreign, and I couldn't stay among them, while people were like rag dolls. I had lost the comfort of life's things, in the rooms and interiors where everything seemed to have a guilty conscience. Rough, cardboard-like, malicious. Reality, which for me no longer coincided with truth, had turned into a calm, waking nightmare.

Working was somehow easier because I was always somewhere else. It wasn't really me scrubbing floors, fluffing pillows, and straightening sheets. I wasn't there when I brushed coats and shoes, cooked lunch for the children, or did the shopping. I was lost in the absurd thought that it would be nice to freeze my mother's body at the creamery, to keep her with me always. In the end, what unsettled me most was that there was nothing left of her to touch. There were times when I fainted without anyone coming to my aid. I was alone in the house, and even if they did return, they left me time to recover on my own.

It was as if the fog of the north had seeped into my head. I vaguely remember the moment I met the butcher's boy, a hazel-colored youth with fierce manners, who showed interest in me right away. I often quivered with a feverish rage and lack of awareness. He had plenty of time to study me, reading who knows what in my empty eyes. If what happened later hadn't occurred, I surely wouldn't remember him now. He was an irregular, an illegal, and lived by slipping through the loose mesh of others' attention. He was a wolf on the hunt, patient. He waited for the right moment, up to one stormy evening. I was hurriedly leaving his shop to take the groceries home, as I'd done mid-week for months, completely absorbed with the thought that I would get soaked.

He quickly maneuvered around the counter, running after me to offer shelter under his umbrella. He started to exchange a few words, listening to the little I had to say with an angelic face and animal-like teeth, staring at me as if from a distance. He asked me to wait a few seconds, freed a red bicycle from its chain, and began walking it beside me. We headed toward the children's house while I clutched the package of meat in my hands. Water and blood trickled down our sides. He asked if he could see me again, and I said no. He left, laughing loudly, just before I opened the door, letting me get at least a little wet on my shoulders and hair.

That night, I was seized by spasms and delirium, unable to distinguish between waking thoughts and dreams. I saw, or perhaps dreamed, the butcher's boy sitting by my bed where I tossed and turned restlessly. He was smoking a cigarette, but in a second he was beside me, leaning back against the wall and lying on my sweat-soaked mattress. He touched my nose and lips with intolerable brazenness. Then we were standing, facing each other, and he bit me just below the eyelashes of my left eye, like the good wolf and butcher that he was.

*

Days passed, but perhaps I didn't notice. One morning—a holiday, though it felt completely nondescript—I was sitting on the edge of my bed, silently sewing the dark collar of my mourning dress. I had noticed the design during the funeral vision and was now trying to reproduce it. I made some progress; knowing that Anna's body was safely buried gave me some peace. I embroidered as I had been taught as a child, almost without blinking, my eyes now dry. A cold, faded sun spread throughout the whole room, and a haunting lullaby in a soft and unknown dialect echoed in the air. A little girl, down in the courtyard. Even though I couldn't understand her words, they disrupted the meticulous mechanical work I was engaged in. Usually I thread the stitches like a series of little sheep to be herded into the pen, stabbing them one by one and then pulling the thread tight. But this time, pained and astonished, I pricked myself. Blood dripped down my index finger. I started to watch the droplets. I felt hunger and pain, and the girl below kept singing, her voice coming and going. I set my work aside and stared at my index finger pointing to the sky, crying. I was suddenly overwhelmed by profound dismay and let myself fall down, crouching on the floor. My skirt framed the soles of my shoes, dragging on the ground. I brought my finger to my mouth and began to suck the drops of blood away. I tasted iron and salt on my tongue and thought of the disease that had carried my mother away. My aunt had reported, in her own words, what the doctors had explained to her. It seemed that my mother had been struck by a lump of wasted, painful flesh. An inexplicably living lump that had grown inside of her. I struggled to imagine what she must have felt, and it terrified me; the fear of pain took me out of myself. It was impossible to know what it must be like to disappear, to die. I shook myself and walked toward the window. I looked down. The little girl seemed even smaller from that distance, rocking up and down on a chair in the middle of the courtyard, clutching its straw seat and staring straight ahead. She was dressed in white, but her little dress seemed to take on the color of the red wooden backrest. Seeing her made my stomach swell, as if I wanted to swallow her whole and make her disappear forever, to silence her once and for all.

My finger wouldn't stop bleeding, so I went to the kitchen and grabbed some ice. I pressed it forcefully against the wound to stop feeling anything.

I've never been very strong; I was skinny and still am, hard and thin like a bamboo cane. But that afternoon, there was nothing left of me but a dark, poorly-put-together object. A ball of flesh had taken my mother away, and I couldn't understand how it could have happened. At some point, the stuff she was made of rebelled, turned against her, massed in her body, and overcame her.

I was born with the talent for learning, for understanding. With little effort I could learn anything. I knew how to learn. I held on like a damp cloth, letting the excess drops slide off, absorbing just enough to begin doing what needed to be done. I've always had wise hands, a mind in my fingers. It's when I face things like this that I don't understand that I can't manage. How can your own flesh eat away at you from the inside? Suddenly I knew with an unsettling certainty that it would soon happen to me too.

I passed the remaining ice over my cheeks, letting it slide down to my earlobes. I recalled that my mother pierced my ears when I was grown, because the original holes had closed up, impudently rejecting all earrings. Where I come from, girls are born with pierced ears, and even if our families had nothing, they still had enough to buy one nice pair of earrings. And so it was with me: my first earrings were a pair of improbably shiny golden spheres. But my earlobes rejected them; Mama took them out to treat the infection, and the holes closed as soon as possible. She simply stopped putting them on me, and I stopped wearing them.

I was the only girl, the only one in the village, whose ears were smooth and clean, without any ornament. Anna complained about it constantly, talking about me as if I weren't there. *Idda avi a fari sempre di testa so, comu so patri.*[10] *Idda*, a foreigner.

My *masculo*, defenseless earlobes, weren't right, and indeed: they earned me my first kiss. His name was Netto, and he was older than me. He kept asking me questions with his eyes. His eyes were warm

---

10   "She always has to do things her own way, like her father."

and lively, his skin the color of wood, his hair black and curled from the salty air. He made me furious. To make things worse, everyone in the village adored him. Netto was always cheerful and irresistible. Night never fell for him; from the dry earth to the dark sky, his laughter rose among the stars, sharp like a dog's yelping. That was the signal—everyone knew to be cheerful. And I was always left out.

Until one afternoon when I was alone, back when Pino still didn't want me with him. Netto was cycling back from the sea, and maybe that's why I would later want a bicycle myself. I was coming from the wheat fields, from our heat and the cicadas, bored. I was cutting back and forth through the air with a dry, broken branch, sulking. I stood still, staring at him as if I'd been slapped. I watched him get off his bicycle, let it fall to the side, and walk toward me. They say opportunity makes the thief, and I was curious to see what Netto was coming to take from me. I followed him with my eyes as he approached. He grabbed my hand and pulled me close. He brushed my face with his large, hot, dark palm. He came so close that I noticed the striking contrast between his strong hands and assertive demeanor and his eyes. So kind they seemed submissive, they were the color of amber resin, including the darker spots which, along with a halo around the iris, gave them a soulful depth. You should know that tonight the sea was wonderfully flat, he confided to me in Italian rather than in our dialect; I didn't fully understand, as I had never yet seen the sea. Gently, Netto slowly turned my face to the side, and I realized he was gathering my dark curls behind my ears. Finally, he kissed my earlobes gently, first one and then the other, lingering long enough for me to shiver. As he pulled away, before leaving, he let slip that I would always be the only one in the village with ears free for kisses.

I don't know if he was foolish enough to repeat what he had said. What I do know is that the very same evening, my mother nearly attacked me, much more violently than he had, holding a needle tightly between her fingers. It was useless to try to run away, to squirm, to slip away like an eel—she had practiced too much on my brother, and there was no escape for me. She forced me to sit and made me hold both ears between ice cubes. She heated the needle in the fire, blew on it and, without shaking, hesitating or wavering, called me to order by piercing my flesh. The next day, I paraded through the village wearing earrings, surrounded by a red, painful halo. Netto never approached me again, but I didn't get angry with my mother; she'd only done what needed to be done.

Without even realizing it, in Catena's kitchen, I brought the ice close to my mouth and then to my teeth, causing a terrible, squeaky discomfort. I passed it gently over my tongue, little by little, and started to chew. Cube after cube, I swallowed the cold in the hope, I think, it would prove just as good an anesthetic for the soul. I felt my head freeze and stopped thinking for a while. Finally. The cold—white, gray, solid or liquid—was the perfect remedy, taking everything away and leaving me pain-free.

As soon as I'd arrived in the city, I'd silently indulged in a private rebellion and freed my ears again, remembering Netto angrily. Thinking of my mother, I now desperately wanted a pair of pearl earrings.

*

The young butcher circled, vulture-like, under my window, sure he'd get at least one carcass. I peeked out from time to time, torn between the terror of being preyed upon and the curiosity of what would happen if I gave in. I wanted to test his patience without risking losing his interest. Sometimes I bit my lips as I passed by the curtains, stopping myself from pulling them aside. I hoped that I could keep him close by rejecting him, experiencing a pleasant discomfort for the first time. I didn't love him, but I knew what this was about—he had chosen me. There was something animal-like about him that I found interesting. In a way, malicious and curt, he felt close to the earth and thus to my heart, to my origins. My life from then on might have the rich, disgusting smell of rotting meat.

It happened while I was cleaning the mirror. My gaze fell on a pair of exquisite pearl earrings left on the marble countertop, set in gold along with a dark, hard stone. I was overcome with despair and with the realization that I couldn't have acted otherwise. I let myself fall onto the chair and turned the earrings over in my fingers. I wondered if butchers' wives owned jewelry. I wasn't a woman, I couldn't imagine myself as a wife and mother. Afflicted by a strange form of infirmity, I was too preoccupied with listening to myself, constantly engaged in the struggle against my own incompleteness. I was a problem for myself. I would have liked to feel strong and whole, like a lady wearing heavy earrings, needing nothing but myself to be happy. I forced the nearly closed holes in my earlobes to try on the ones in my hands. Suffering as the posts pierced through my flesh seemed like the right thing to do. I felt the warmth of my skin and the blood pulsing, with a ritualistic beat, in my ears. It takes so little to become a lady, without being anything at all. Anna would have been happy, she might even have envied me. I didn't even look at myself in the mirror; I tore the earrings off and slipped them into my pockets. Then I felt disgusted with myself, recognizing the triteness of my hungry gesture, and pulled them out to look at them again. A lady doesn't steal and, if she does, she makes it look respectable. I put the earrings back down.

A faint voice of broken glass, singing a childish nursery rhyme suddenly echoed from the barely-cracked door behind me. The little girl looked at me like a cat, unmoving, her hand still on the handle. Adorable in her blue dress, blonde hair tied in a high ponytail, she moved her mouth like a wooden puppet held up by a bunch of strings. She approached slowly, still singing, and fell silent.

Then she asked me if she could do the same, try on her mother's earrings. I refused, seized by an inexplicable jealousy, as irritated as if they had taken away my favorite doll from my hands.

"Then I'll tell Mama you were playing with her earrings and put them in your pockets because you wanted to take them," she threatened, as children do. For a second her blue eyes seemed black, and I found myself shaking.

I didn't even try to convince her not to do it, I'd never have begged her. I wanted to tear her dress and pull out her hair. I shuddered at the glitter of her pretty necklace; she so small and sparkling, me already grown and bare. I wanted to find a way to humiliate her but instead remained powerless, slumped like a tired old woman. The lace around her little shoes reminded me of foam at the mouth of rabid dogs. I wanted her to hurt. To me, children have always been ambiguous creatures, gifted at once with terrible power and bewildering innocence.

I myself had been a naughty child, I knew children's hearts lacked pity because they had no sense of responsibility, no idea of the future. In her shoes, I'd have done the same to get what I wanted.

As promised, she went to her mother and reported that I was a thief. The evidence that no pieces were missing from the family collection didn't matter; it was enough that the girl had seen me slip them in the fold of my dress for a moment. It was a questioning of motives.

That's when I learned that ladies' trust works just like an endemic disease, it gets passed easily and so exhausts itself following an identical course. No one could trust me anymore, they would truly have liked to, but I'd gotten myself into trouble with my own hands. They also pointed out how they had entrusted their children to me, proof of how they held no prejudices. They explained that real ladies do not pay attention to insignificant things like geographical origin, but that I myself had confirmed the malicious rumors circulating about my people.

I'd lost my job and Catena her evening stories. We'd both had to withdraw, just a bit, toward the point we'd started from.

*

To the butcher I was still fresh meat. Indeed, I had the impression that my stunt, which I hadn't even committed, had won me new respect in his eyes. The same thing had happened before with Pino; he must have seen something in me that the other girls couldn't give him: a partner in wrongdoing and illegality. Like Netto, the butcher had tousled hair and nails that looked like shiny almond slices, and that's why I liked him. One could almost say he was handsome. He also had a bicycle, which encouraged me, and so he convinced me. He, on the other hand, was persuaded by the misunderstanding that led him to believe I was a thief and a swindler.

Since he was a child, the butcher had dreamed of making movies, in front of or behind the camera, but he'd been cursed with that incurable cancer: lack of talent. So he contented himself with taking me to see movies. He'd pay for my ticket, and we'd sit close together in the darkness. I enjoyed closing my eyes to focus on the sound of heels clicking on the asphalt coming from the screen. In silence, neither of us reached out to the other. He took me pedaling hard, making me sit on the handlebars, and I let him work hard, imagining the tension in his calves and thighs, the weight on his lungs. Love must have been all the pain he felt in his muscles, the sweat down his back. I'd grown used to and then fond of the closeness of his body, I didn't know what more was needed, I couldn't imagine what else being together might mean. I wasn't interested in the future, but in the constant present, I asked for a good memory and endurance, and hands ready for hard work. I myself wouldn't have been able to give him anything different.

He took me to the butcher shop and taught me the trade, letting me watch him in front of the counter and behind it, where the stench was almost unbearable. I helped him move buckets full of giblets and blood, small and black like a fly among all the rest. I became familiar with knives and different types of cuts and with the toughness of fibrous meat. I learned what it means to put strength into your shoulder, elbow, and wrist, how steady your fingers must remain. My mood resembled those blades. As a child, I'd learned to keep my father's accounts, so the butcher sometimes tasked me with serving the customers who came to shop: I myself had once been one of them. I realized that the trade was profitable, it dirtied your smock but filled your belly. Being brutal paid off. Cruelty suited my butcher, who was swift in his movements, agile and powerful with his fingers. He'd never make it in the movies, but his was a story to admire.

On my part, I liked being ready for a man's job. I didn't let myself falter for a second, I didn't want to ask questions, I carried on, sure that being good, being the best at a male job would make me desirable. In the evenings, I rapidly jotted down everything I'd learned, so as not to forget. I was crafting a manual that would be useless to me: Catena had made it clear she wouldn't allow me to be a scullery maid in a foul-smelling shop. If I so desired, I'd be the butcher's wife and nothing more.

I was born at the end of winter. For my birthday, the butcher gave me a silver locket that he'd had engraved with a tulip. He said I should wear it from then on. Flowers are given to beautiful women, he laughed, adding with a smirk that since I was a thief, he'd chosen the least precious one for me, a scentless flower that dies before spring.

I wasn't used to gifts, nor to wearing necklaces. Its weight felt unpleasant on my breastbone and skin, where the locket exchanged its warmth. Like a tongue torturing a cut lip to chase a pleasant sting, I tortured the silver with my fingers throughout the day. I was there all the time, dragging my thoughts along, constantly revolving around the young meat man who wanted me powerfully. His bones had become dear to me, his pungent smell of bread and fresh oranges in the sun. While I was waiting to find a new job, I passed the hours not spent with him at the cinema or in the butcher shop or the evenings in Catena's company seated at a table in a bar with sad walls and a faded, pitiful clientele. I'd order a glass of fresh milk and a cup of black coffee, and I'd work on my manual. Ever since I was a little girl, I shouldn't have written what I wrote. Now it was just that I had decided to furnish with detailed drawings the things I reported to myself with detailed drawings, in order to reinforce my memory. Leafing through the dense pages of procedures, notes, and observations, I slipped down into the raw intestines of beasts. My legs felt dead, but I allowed myself bright thoughts.

*

A few months later, Catena managed to find me a job as a telephone operator. It wasn't too hard; I had a secure position as the daughter of a war martyr, even though my father had never really been a soldier. I only had one photo of him, which I always carried with me. It showed a young man moving baskets on a field, his back bent, a mountain of long, dark hair tousled by the wind, his amused gaze fixed in the eyes of the observer, in my eyes. A thick mustache framed his mouth, twisted in a mocking smirk.

On the first day, they gave me a knee-length black apron with a white collar. We were all women, organized into groups, all with a church-like and orderly appearance. We covered the morning and afternoon shifts and found ourselves free again after seven hours. The men had been given the night shift, which I'd have preferred and would have covered enthusiastically, because at night I was alert and awake. We never saw the men, hearing only their voices running along the wires and ordering us numbers to connect to by plugging them into the switchboard. We worked in a room of plugs.

We quickly learned to recognize customers, especially those with sordid tales of illicit affairs. We'd gather in a tight group, listening awestruck to the clandestine lovers whispering in each other's ears. The room would fall silent as a tomb, silent as marble, sometimes interrupted by an excited giggle from someone who couldn't contain her thrills and embarrassment. The switchboard was my sentimental education; I studied there to learn about other people's love. Too many words wasted chasing the feeling, which seemed to me as though one should merely experience it. My butcher would never have spoken to me in a low voice and didn't use sweet words to lure his prey into the net. He was tired veins, the sound of iron, the smell of a pit. He was my silent celebration, a joy that couldn't be spokenand that we didn't speak.

I was happy to send part of my salary to my aunt. I felt the warmth, which was curled up and dormant in my stomach, turn itself and register the change, I felt grown up. I'd always been very aware of myself, but in a penitential way, whereas now I felt I was beginning to understand and even like myself. I bought a pair of shoes and two dresses, I started taming my curls and my eyes, so dark you couldn't see the irises. Makeup came easily to me; I quickly learned a style that more or less pleased me. I followed the line of my eye with the brush, then swiftly curved it upward, quivering slightly to avoid spreading the bristles and smudging the color all over my eyelid. Catena laughed at me, calling me a wild cat. I was relieved that it was noticeable.

As I had been at school, I was alone, but I didn't feel that way. I had no desires that extended beyond myself; I was content and didn't want to share myself. I continued to be oil that doesn't mix with water. I felt a sense of depth sharing space with others, but my head felt heavy. I knew I was unusually quiet; I worked hard and well, silently. My locket was the only company I could tolerate, after so long enduring it. I thought about the butcher's ankles, wrists, knees, pelvis, and neck, so solid it couldn't be broken. And me with him. I was obsessed with the sad and unjust thought that, like every living thing, he too would die one day.

Without my wanting it and, in fact, completely against my will, a girl at the office began to like me. Since no one appeared able to resist her open character, I became a challenge for her. Agnese was cheerful, light-hearted, silly, completely scattered, and out of touch with herself, my exact opposite. She was a pleasant and attractive woman, fair-skinned and fair-spirited, blonde and full of good intentions. I didn't like her at all, I couldn't stand being around her. She wanted to save me, and it felt like a violation, arousing deep suspicion within me. She was a light that cast no shadow, a beacon that confuses you; my balance was drawn in the dimness of the film or under the lab lamp. I described her in detail to my butcher's apprentice. We smiled and fantasized about cutting her into pieces; he focused on explaining how we should proceed, which tools would make as little of a mess as possible. It would have been nice to sell her to the neighborhood ladies, always looking for the choicest meat.

*

It was no joke; meeting Agnese was like an earthquake for me. She persisted in her effort to win me over, and even though I wanted to destroy her, I dreamed instead of being attacked by a wild feline that chased me for hours until it finally caught up with me, crushing my bones between its teeth. I woke up breathless, terrified of having to go to work.

I confided in Catena, asking for advice, this time without smiling. We were having dinner, sipping warm broth while she shook her head in disbelief, seeking support from her husband, who was absorbed in reading a newspaper that seemed to be holding him captive. I'd never heard him speak. He remained silent, despite Catena asking him multiple times if it wasn't truly dreadful to be forced to spend all one's time in the company of such a pest. Catena waited for an answer, her head tilted to one side like a curious bird. Her husband was one of those men who believed they wore the pants but who could barely manage to button them in the morning. Convinced they are in control, they can't handle more than four sheets of newspaper to skim through at breakfast. Catena was the Southern woman who managed everything, silently. And it was she who answered me:

"It is, and very much so," she said decisively. She understood me.

While we washed the dishes that evening, Catena paused and told me she knew what had to be done. She gripped the edge of the sink tightly, aware that it wasn't the nicest solution. Initially, I was disappointed upon hearing her plan.

Patrhe, figghiu, e spiritu santu,[11] she said, you have to use salt. Salt was the most effective method possible. She asked me to sit down and placed a plate of white grapes and a loaf of bread on the table. Grapes and bread should be eaten together, creating an unexpected pleasure in your mouth. Enjoying the sweet and salty flavors of this poor man's treat, Catena explained it to me.

She took the example of her grandmother, threatened with eviction. She was being punished for not being willing to give up a room to the landlord, who'd decided to expand his apartments. The poor old woman didn't know what to do, so she waited until nighttime. Catena emphasized that she thought carefully before acting, repeating over and over that certain things shouldn't be done lightly. But the woman had eventually made up her mind; she crossed herself and went out. She sprinkled salt on the landlord's doormat, adding a few ritual phrases in case some extra help was needed. The next day, the man was found lifeless, his skin shriveled, frozen in a pose of rivulsion in the armchair of his spacious living room, which apparently hadn't been big enough for him. His end wasn't that of a righteous man; death had frightened him before taking him away.

So, Catena, sure I wouldn't find an alternative, suggested doing the same with Agnese. The request needed to be measured well; nothing fatal would happen, but I'd be able to get rid of her. Only then did I remember how Catena thought she had found a husband. Catena read my face and added that magic works for those who believe. Faith is a complex matter, rewarding only those who have the courage to persevere, and, with Christian charity, it plucks from the fire the last,

---

11   "By the Father, Son, and Holy Spirit."

the damned, the bad, and the inept because everyone else can manage on their own. Catena gave me a bag of salt and recommended I think about it. The following weeks convinced me I had to try, if only because Catena's plan was by far easier to put into practice than the butcher's.

I carried the salt with me, not really knowing what to do with it. The idea struck me at lunchtime when I was forced one too many times to sit next to Agnese. I thought about what I'd say when the moment came. I wouldn't sprinkle the salt on her carpet or behind her shoes; I wouldn't throw it at her because I didn't know how to perform complex magic. I'd poison her food, with the simple aim of taking away her taste and pleasure. As soon as I could, I poured Catena's salt into Agnese's dish, making sure no one saw me. Agnese began to eat, and I smiled at her. She lit up, believing for a moment that she'd won me over. Her body relaxed just enough for me to properly enjoy the next impact. I'm sure she imagined long conversations and a budding friendship, which served only to confirm her good heart and impeccable conduct. I was proof that she was a good person: she was kind, even to me. I watched the light in her cheeks disappear into a dark shadow. Her eyes stilled for a moment and, within seconds, her once pretty, fair face crumpled under my gaze. It looked like her hair turned gray. She transformed as if I'd tortured her for hours—which, deep down, was what I wanted to do to everyone who flaunted their goodness. She opened her mouth to throw up, but nothing came out. It was then that I leaned in to whisper Forget me, so she wouldn't forget. I terrified her the way only senseless things can. Like laundry detergent, Catena's salt had removed the stain without leaving a trace.

I ran out of the office like a fury, stuffing the remaining salt packet into my coat pocket. Once I felt I was far enough away, I collapsed onto a bench, still breathing heavily. I didn't know what had upset me so, perhaps it was the weight and exhaustion following a battle. I just wanted to be left in peace, not ever to learn how to behave myself.

I looked around: without realizing it, I had ended up in front of a church bulging with domes, accessible via a portico like that of an ancient temple. High up on the left you could still see the signs of a bombing. In the city, it was known as a sanctuary of consolation. I wondered if this referred more to the café across the street, which revitalized the spirits of a line of fur-coated ladies on a perpetual pilgrimage. As is often the case among Catholics, they mixed pleasure with pain, gulping down delicious hot chocolate that scalded the palate.

A man in a suit and tie crossed the square diagonally, intersecting the path of two nuns in blue habits. Next to the entrance of the church, at the foot of the small staircase, a boy lay on the ground looking at the sky. One thing about the big city that both repulsed and reassured me was the freedom to be nobody, to be alone, lacking nothing, with no needs. I envied that boy, whose life was contained within the lineaments of his body. I, on the other hand, was caught up in the terrifying blackmail that comes with relating to others; I was victim and executioner alike, shunning expectations. Others were too much for me, not a simple group but each one a dark aggregate of longings, preseumptions, and demands.

My forehead burned; my underarms, beneath my knees, in the crease of my elbows, around my heels, an unbearable heat stained my clothes, and I began hallucinating. Frozen by a deep agitation, I writhed in a pointless neurosis. I don't know how long the crisis lasted; I woke abruptly, shaken by a police officer. I must have been in a terrible state, my skin yellow and still sweating. The guard mistook me for a homeless person and worriedly told me I had to leave, I couldn't stay there. I turned confusedly to my left and saw the bag I had placed in my pocket spilling out, Catena's salt scattered on the gray ground around me.

Back home, I locked myself in the bathroom and began cutting away the white of my nails until I reached raw flesh, in a mix of satisfaction and pain. Away with all the excess. I prepared a hot bath and let the room fill with steam. I felt my heart pulsing under my fingertips. My makeup had run so much my eyes were hollow; I shivered with cold despite sweating from head to neck and in my hair. I filled a basin with water and soap for my clothes and undressed. I immersed everything I had on and began scrubbing hard, raising a cloud of foam. As I felt my feet hurt on the cold floor, I let my arms drop and waited a few moments, holding back tears. My head bowed, I approached the bathtub and got in. It was almost funny how little room my body took up, displacing a ridiculous amount of water, but I had let the tap run too long and a trickle spilled over the edges and onto the tiles.

I stared ahead at the white ceramic tiles. A warm film began to form on the surface. It would soon come off in fat drops. I waited, ready to enjoy the sudden roll. Watching the drops, I waited for them to swell. Once they were full, down they went, falling quickly. That's when I heard a knock on the door.

I asked who it was, and on the other side, Catena said It's me. I invited her in. In a thin voice, she asked if she could come closer, already sitting down beside me. I nodded yes. She must have sensed something and asked me about the salt.

"It worked," I said seriously, without mentioning that some of the bag had spilled at my feet. Realizing something was wrong, Catena became alarmed, her face tinged with concern. She put a hand on my forehead and then asked to check the hollows of my eyes. Without saying a word, she got up and closed the door behind her. She returned shortly after, gripping a mug of hot water where she'd steeped bitter lemon rinds. She stirred a dollop of honey with a spoon to make it dissolve more quickly. Trying without much success to be reassuring, she sat back down on the edge of the tub, giving me a forced smile and urging me to drink up. I hesitated, so she jokingly warned me, as if I were a stubborn child, that *avissi avuto a chiamari u mericu*[12] if I refused. She gave me time to blow away the steaming heat, then turned serious. Catena wasn't the type to give explicit lessons. That day, however, she told me that I shouldn't make others fear me; I needed to appear fragile, naive. If all goes well, no one will bother you; if someone *avissi a fariti male*,[13] I wouldn't surprise them ever enough.

Contrary to what people in the village said, Catena was no joke gone wrong. Catena had been a wild girl like me. She'd just grown up, gotten older, and hidden, as I'd have to learn to do myself. But she was always there.

She turned her back to me and started scrubbing my clothes, which I hadn't finished washing. She wrung them out and shook them before

---

12 "She'd have to call the doctor."

13 "Tries to hurt you."

hanging them up. She turned off the light and closed the door, even though I was still in the water; I think she wanted to give me some rest and a break. The butcher filled my thoughts.

*

The only thing that truly moves me are blood ties, having a past in common. Anna hadn't visited me in a few months; her memory was vivid but set in stone. I slept little but without dreaming, and if I did, I saw an endless expanse of golden wheat fields. I was able to manage my memories like healthy people do, even with melancholy. It was like my father had never existed. I remembered Pino and started to whistle; I couldn't help but cry. But that was normal, I was normal. I had a far-off family, a home, a friend, a job and a man who was like me. I didn't want to be where I was; I didn't want to be what I was, but I knew I couldn't stay a barefoot girl from the South. I was at peace, resigned to the fact that I had what was expected of someone my age. Anna would never have bet on it.

Adult life imposes an order and constancy that weren't in my nature but which I now possessed as if I'd bought them at the market. You get used to everything in time; sometimes I even thought I was happy.

You fall asleep one starless night following a clear and warm day. You're tense and sweaty, young, all soft, damp, light flesh. You wake up one rainy morning, years later. Time seemed to pass slowly, yet looking back, it's as if someone had erased it. Taking it away from you, swiftly and sharply. Three weeks barely have time to become a month, and then, all of a sudden, it was already months ago, many years ago.

*

The butcher's boy had advanced in his career and now ran the shop on his own. Thinking about his boss, I reflected that you should never hire someone to teach them skills with a knife: when he deems the time has come, he'd know how to remove you from the world. I couldn't rule out that that's what had happened.

74

And so I became the butcher's wife. After an initial period of carefree dating, it was decided that the matter should be formalized. We moved into a building not far from where Catena lived, but very different from her lovely home. I found myself in one of those gray rectangles far from the center, made for those of us came from down South, for those who had respectable work, who could afford a basic apartment and therefore lacked for nothing. We both had a salary; a modern house seemed the most desirable goal to us. To the great disappointment of the butcher, who more and more wanted something to call his own, we didn't yet make enough money to buy it. Month after month, year after year, he repeated that things would soon change and that one day we'd be able to afford a house of our own. For him, being a man meant purchasing power over everything, a world within the reach of his pocket and his will. He'd been taught that you stop being a son when you begin working, you're no longer a child when you get married, you become a man when you're in charge. On my part, I began to understand that uncertainty doesn't pertain exclusively to youth. I also knew that I'd feel like a stranger anywhere other than within the four stone walls back in the village. Those walls belonged to no one; they rose from the earth, and they belonged to us because we had always belonged to them, simply because we were part of the same natural place.

The butcher and I didn't speak much to each other, until we finally stopped altogether. Fifteen years passed, and it was a sterile love, maybe it was my fault given that I knew how to attract men, but I wasn't capable of creating them. I don't have the key to this secret, nor can I describe it; motherhood had pushed me back into the world of men. I was never able to sculpt anyone's features.

Persuaded by his neat, straight, white teeth, at first I thought I was marrying a gentleman, a man with whom *t'arrizzetti, bedda abbissata*[14] forever, and so on to another level. I saw it as a satisfactory agreement between equals, an understanding like the one I'd had with Pino. Instead, they say to take a wife it's like a theft, in a best-case scenario a transaction. Like my mother, I was taken by the wrong man.

---

14   "you will settle down nicely."

Hate and contempt didn't come immediately, no. For some time, I believe we did manage to love each other or, rather, to want each other, often locked in a raging full-body struggle. We waited, as is proper, until marriage but regretted it as soon as we were allowed to touch each other. His warm mouth seemed the holiest thing I'd ever encountered. I'd become a tamed animal, living an anxious life in captivity, waiting to be caressed.

I took pleasure in imagining that we were survivors. Maybe others, in distant houses, also dreamed of being the last ones standing, feeling special in the end—the strongest, the healthiest. I imagined the epidemic returning like when I was a child, all the stores closed, their windows shattered on the asphalt, the interiors empty and sad, looted within hours. This gave meaning to his hungry hands and thirsty skin. I fantasized about twisted stomachs, painfully consumed from within. No appetite except for each other; we were all need. Finally, I dreamed that the epidemic wouldn't defeat us, and then we'd die of hunger, but we'd die together, barricaded like resistance fighters within our white walls on the fourth floor. Both born elsewhere, grown up elsewhere, dying there together, of hunger. Feeling was the only thing left—pain, fear, the faint pleasure of tired sex, his sweet scent mixed with the stench of death, the odor rising from the street. This fantasy consumed my mind to such an extent that I once found myself twirling a knife between my fingers, imagining I could use it for us. A work tool turned magical, powerful talisman. I placed it on the nightstand, and as he kissed me, the thought glimmered in the corner of my eye. He licked my lips, and he smelled good, our room a drifting raft, all bed. Tenderly, I realized he could eat me. I would lengthen his life, but then he'd be alone, waiting.

It may have lasted years, a spiral with no escape, just us. It felt as if it were nailed to my forehead, a constant thought. It felt ridiculous for him to be separate from me, and I knew he felt the same. Need kept us alive and united. We couldn't create life; we consumed each other, and it wasn't necessarily a good thing. Our bond both sustained and exhausted us. It sucked our life away, demanded it for itself; there was no room for anyone else. We loved each other, but we weren't loving; we sought each other, but we weren't able to care for one another. Our love was a love of the flesh, of need. In the end, I found myself with the fortune Anna had always wished for herself. Anna couldn't have imagined that my fortune was also a punishment. For one reason or another, we never manage to be content.

*

I don't know how you can forget something like that but you can, because that's what happened to the butcher. All of a sudden, I was nothing to him, except for an irritating hindrance, an abuse of his independence. I was alone once more, in my own home. Perhaps our encounters of living flesh lied on his behalf, making him appear thoughtful when he wasn't. To be honest, my own passion was dead skin; after slaughtering so many animals, even he was nothing more than a standing corpse. My husband had no family; I was surprised by the very thought that he could have ever had one. He came from nowhere and no one. I thought he'd take root in me, the only one capable of perfectly matching him. But the butcher existed on earth like a stone, with no sap to exchange. He let himself be kicked around, not even knowing why, by whom or where to. He deluded himself into thinking it was a form of freedom. I'd let myself be seduced and convinced by the idea that I would be complete and emptied in someone who had nothing in common with me except the will to be together. Completing yourself in someone else is a mistake, the only true scandal I've committed in my life. Although it's only with someone else that you lack for nothing, you inevitably end up lacking everything.

I was unwell because my body was suffering. The pain appeared as a dull ache that consumed me physically. Every evening, a glass of water, a taste of mint and acid. I dissolved a painkiller, which I was abusing to calm my head. I remember the toxic powder spreading in a gray cloud that seemed unhealthier than my illness.

My life was complicated; I started using the night again. It wasn't easy to be me. I felt hardened, slept a handful of hours on a bed of nails. I ate just enough to not disappear, brushing the guilt from my hair. I vividly remember the last time I thought of him with kindness. I was in the bedroom, motionless, trapped by an unusual thought. There was a grate in the wall, but what was it for? Looking at it drove me crazy. I stood on tiptoe on a chair, not even knowing what I wanted to do. I was face to face with the grate, the chair wobbled under my feet, fidgeting to go away to who knows where. I might have even been able to float there, just to remain and stare at it. The grate. I looked into the filthy darkness of the wall's interior. I turned my head, pressed my ear against it, and closed my eyes. It was a pitch-black tunnel; I pictured it connected to my butcher's stomach, leading straight to his warm navel. When he spoke, that's where he spoke from, from the middle, from the breaking point, from the exact center of the highest and lowest inclinations. I had my ear on the belly of the monster, my assassin, and it was so tender.

These weren't dark thoughts because the sun was shining outside, and everything with it could only shine. I was shining too, standing on the chair with a vacant stare. If I had suddenly disappeared, only the room would have known, keeping the secret without telling anyone. I sat down and lit a damp, useless cigarette that didn't draw well. I'd stolen it to try the pleasures Pino and Anna used to enjoy, but it disgusted me. My fingers shook. I thought about the butcher's sparse beard and his perpetually puzzled expression, how he moved his lips oddly, never quite believing what he said, occasionally revealing the cruel glint of his teeth. I lived with him and didn't know how tall he was, but I remembered the outline of his hands well. Why think about eyes, teeth, and hands, the circle of his wrists, ears, feet? It was simple and trite to feel so much interest in another's body, which is just flesh, bones and scraps, a carcass. Why are we tormented by the image of a throbbing vein on a forehead, the space between teeth, the color of a tongue, as if it were something special? Mixed with a sense of nausea, I felt an unexpected tenderness unsuited to my condition.

I looked outside. Some have preferred to go to America , but they don't know that on the outskirts of our North, where I lived, America exists, and I've seen it. I lived on the edge of the city, a border area. The lavish villas of the new rich faced the high-rise blocks of public housing, with only a long row of trees in between. Behind all of us were fields of corn and tall grass. A breeze of chlorine wafted over from the pools on the other side of the road; some lucky people had a portico in front of their doorway, where they had placed a large, multi-colored umbrella. I will never cross the ocean to see another thing like that.

*

One rainy afternoon, he was in a corner of the kitchen. He held the bread against his chest and drew the knife toward himself, managing to create paper-thin slices. I desperately wished he'd cut himself, wished he'd wither away. He deserved to have all the deep darkness he threw on me to be spat back in his face, for it to drown him, to carry him away.

*

One of the last days, I found him wrapping a small box with careful hands and a silly grin. I spied on him from the half-open door, he didn't notice me at first. He jumped like a cat when he suddenly felt me behind him and saw me. I asked what it was, and he said nothing. I insisted, but he kept claiming there was nothing to see. Finally, he said with a sweet smile, as frightening as if he'd attacked me, maybe it's a surprise for you. I never got the chance to open that little box because I never received it.

I've often wondered what might have been inside. I'm sure now that it was a silver flower for someone to wear around her neck. I'd wearied him; he repeated the same moves of a clever hunter, trying to find someone who was me, but I wasn't the one. Sick with permanent dissatisfaction, my husband was, first and foremost, dissatisfied with himself.

Keeping a promise for life seems to be hard. For me, it came as naturally as having two legs, two arms, and a head on my shoulders. I don't know how else to say it; I was devoted to him. Despite having come to detest him, to feel pain in his presence, I didn't know how to live otherwise, nor did I want to. I never wanted to escape; it was easier to imagine his death than my own. I would never have killed myself voluntarily, following my family's path. I wanted to affirm myself and our agreement. The promise I'd made haunted me. I had expected pain; Catena had warned me. It was a pact that couldn't be broken, one that matters in every case. I remembered this and carried on, because I'd given my word. His illnesses were mine, his obsessions were ours. We had the same germ in our heads, thin bodies that fit together like the gears of a machine. Having loved each other had been a bonus; we were, in any case, a destiny to be fulfilled. Love might come back.

*

I should have realized it that morning, but it's not easy to walk the path the leads to an end. I was washing tomatoes in an acid-green colander, a red stain danced before my eyes like a premonition of misfortune. I should have realized it while I was biting into the scarlet spheres, which tasted of pain and defeat. I had a premonition but ignored it. I didn't feel it coming, and the blow shook me from head to toe.

Back from work, my butcher looked guilty, asked me to sit at the kitchen table, he said he needed to talk to me. He sat down too, clasped his hands, looked down. He opened his mouth several times but couldn't speak. He soon gave up on consideration for me, any lies, let his gaze turn calm and then sharp. And said simply that it was over. He was leaving me the house, as gentlemen do in these situations with a woman. He shrugged it off with a sigh, the worst was over for him. He looked calmly out the window, toward America.

It was only then that I realized how little he possessed; within a few minutes, he'd gathered his things and was ready to vanish. He vanished. Rolled away.

Three words and the rest of my life began, a wound never healed by time, the terror of a child with eyes wide open in the dark of the night. The anguish of being alone tormenting the skin.

Time doesn't heal betrayed love, just as it doesn't heal a deep scar. Like someone with a gash on their face who spends days bleeding, suffering from stitches, vomiting at night, sweating cold, changing bandages for months as they recall the beast that sank its claws into their flesh, then wakes up one morning to find the wound no longer bleeding, not life-threatening, the infections are gone, all that's left is an annoying ache. Day after day, they're increasingly sure their time on this earth isn't over, but no amount of months or years will wash away the wound from their face, the fear and anguish of seeing themselves disfigured every day in the mirror. This was me, from that moment on, forevermore.

Speaking of a love that's over isn't sentimental or pathetic. It's telling a story of war and death. Those who suffered before me tried to explain it, saying they felt their heart breaking, and when I think about it, I still feel the pain of when mine broke. I can feel the bile churning, my guts tearing. I was born and raised to be with him, we grew up together, yet now I was losing my meaning, I was dissolving.

I, who'd never believed in God, approached love in a religious way. I'd been as faithful as a nun, capable of giving my all, even in exchange for nothing. I'd loved my father, then my brother. The only loves I had known were blood ties, which death had torn from me. Like a son, like a brother, like a father I had loved him, as if he were of my own blood, as if our bond couldn't be broken, as if we could never tire of it. I'd made a mistake, I had built my world with a fickle, superficial man, who did nothing but improvise. He was alive, who knows where, without me.

My flesh, nails, hair remained, but I was nothing anymore, a heap of shapeless pain, killed by abandonment. My mother had been right that being a woman carries a dirty curse: the fate of abandonment. I dreamed every night, and I dreamed we were together, but I was the other woman, and together we laughed at me. I cried all my tears, went back to being hard as stone, I never loved again.

I shouted for as long as I had heart, body, voice. I shouted within our white walls, which saw me slip from happiness into the foul pit where I was drowning. Patiently the lime swallowed my cries of pain. A curse on you. A curse on you, that you may never find peace. Catena had taught me to believe in curses: I hoped a sickness would grow inside my husband, turning into a monster to kill him with a bite, when he was gray and sad. I pictured killing him without lifting a finger, in accordance with law and nature, just unleashing my betrayed love against him—the depth of a feeling which, worn inside out, is a weapon of deadly power. I rediscovered an age-old strength within me. As a child, my father would pick me up and, smiling, teach me that you have to take what you want resolutely. He brought me near a fig tree and said that you won't get the fruit by sitting under the branches with your mouth open. He made me reach out, forcefully detach the fruit from the plant, severing their contact. We split the fig in half, red as the blood of a losing soldier, and shared it.

The butcher had left me, all that remained was to kill him. I pondered my husband's death at length, I dreamed of killing him slowly, with my thoughts. He would have done better to love me, it would have saved his life. I've often wondered if he's ever felt the burning of my absence in the empty chambers of his soul. Who knows if he's ever wondered where life has taken me, how I move my hands while speaking or folding a sheet, if I've ever laughed heartily without him, how I've decided to wear my hair. I'd like to know if he's ever wished to come back to me.

*

If I weren't still here, I would swear I stopped breathing. I slid slowly down the muddy tunnels of magical thinking; for months I counted every move, choreographed my actions, believing this would help me bring him home. I gave up coffee, as my mother had done when Pino fell ill. One loss in exchange for another, I wanted to see him come back. I told myself, count to ten while washing these dishes, if you manage to clean them, he'll come back. Or else, he won't come back if you can't keep this plant alive. Unlike curses, my spells didn't work; I completed every task I set myself, yet he didn't return. I possess a dark strength that can break everything, but I have no fertile ground within me.

It was his job, I made no difference, he'd simply cleaned a dead animal, taken everything from me down to the bone. He'd set me aside and, whistling, had moved on to another carcass. Even when I finally surrendered to an exhausted sleep, I managed to grant myself a sweet thought: I'll be yours forever, for this you shall perish.

Revenge is often spoken of with scowling eyes and a dark heart, as if it were something deserving only of contempt. I disagree; revenge is geometry, it's attention, it's memory, it's resilience. I, who have been revenge, who am revenge, speak of it with joy; my brow becomes smooth and luminous. Revenge is a powerful, solid emotion, fuel for life; it doesn't consume, but sustains. It requires feeling, courage, strategy. It's not for those who can't love, for those who don't remember. Let forgiveness be left to the forgetful, to the weak of heart. Those who seek revenge after a pain that breaks their knees and kidneys regain depth and fiber, fluid circulating through their own muscles.

A vengeful person is not an envious one forced into inactivity by incapacity, nor a villain the way he was, light-hearted and with no reason. If I'd still been with Pino, we'd have plotted playfully behind his back, we'd have found a way to make him pay while laughing. Left alone, I faced my pain like the purest diamond; it pierced me, it looked through me, but it didn't break me. After all, devoting your life to hating your enemy is a form of love.

WINTER

I envy people who are afraid, for they know when to stop. I wish I'd
had someone by my side to tell me when enough was enough. I was
hurting myself, I was angry. I hadn't been enough, it had to be my
fault. My mother had made my father run away, and I hadn't been
able to make him stay. I'd done the same with my husband, there must
have been something wrong with me.

For other women, a man represented life, love, commitment, the
measure by which they were judged. I gave and demanded loyalty. I
wanted him alive, as a friend, as a partner. In the end, for different
reasons, I'd made the same fatal mistake as my peers: I'd made him
my destiny. None of us cared about happiness; we cared about having
a man. Otherwise, we would be good-for-nothings, passing from too
young to too old without even noticing, spoiled for everyone and
everything worthwhile.

I found myself a victim of dog-like loyalty and now I foamed
at the mouth with rage, ready to tear the world apart, growling and
biting everything. I don't know if I was suffering from the loss of love
or of pride, or if simply the body with which I shared every space had
grown smaller, my body that by this time was an extension of myself.

When you love someone who's no longer there, you wish all their
things would disappear with them. It's unbearable to see any piece
of cloth that touched their skin or a book they held. If they take
everything with them, leaving an empty house, they're a thief and a
scoundrel. What's left is only good for moaning over.

My soul was a fragile thread. I lived in darkness, the strong light
of lamps might have killed me. I smoked dozens of cigarettes a day

with disgust, yet taking pleasure in my raspy coughs and the gray deposits in my lungs. Like a perverse delight, I smoked one after another, sometimes lighting two at once, letting them burn down to the filter in the ashtray. I ate until I was sick, fantasizing about becoming deformed, then threw up, sobbing from the effort, feeling catastrophe in my heart and sweat on my temples. I forced myself to go to the movies, as we did when we were young. I didn't pay attention, I just wanted to suffer as much as possible. I began to understand my mother, who had punished herself to hurt others.

Being hurt doesn't mean you've been torn apart, no matter how much it feels that way, no matter what you believe. If you maintain a human shape and move on your own feet, love hasn't killed you, and that's where the horror lies: in rediscovering your strength, that you're still there despite the pain. I decided to stop eating, challenging my natural thinness to push itself toward the unimaginable. I smoked with displeasure and drank, having learned that if you don't touch food, drinking and smoking first bring pleasure and then terrible suffering. I lost weight and drank, I lost and lost, all of myself, so that there was nothing left but a mild and altered mind. The triteness of the everyday had become raw flesh suffering from the touch of an insensitive hand, rubbing and rubbing. It burns. Being alive in the way of nature, with neither love nor peace, constantly exposed, frightened, forcibly vigilant. Ready for the possibility of being eaten alive. Time treated me strangely. So slow as to become painful, it slipped away day after day, which took place for me as if I were living someone else's life. Unable to communicate my pain, I cradled it jealously late at night, my eyes lost out the window on the neighborhood, the palms of my hands abandoned on my knees, facing up. I was the portrait of my mother. Like Anna, I had become skinned alive.

I wished Pino were with me, killing lizards with hot stones, feeling truly bad, lighthearted like all wicked people, indifferent to everything. I dreamed of Pino taking me to the sea. Through a web of mist over my eyes, I saw the beach and heard the water calling in the distance. Like when we were *picciriddi*,[15] a lack of sleep came back to haunt

---

15   Children, little kids.

me. The I of childhood is, perhaps, the only true I that we say we've outgrown as we mature. I've never felt so truly myself until, as an adult, I recognized who I used to be in myself, feeling again as I did in the beginning.

Insomnia, my only companion during those days, you saved me, torturing me, from oblivion. You forced me into a state of lucid alertness, the deaf and shaking drunkenness of someone who just can't fall asleep and thus doesn't completely dissolve, melting into the deep sky's flickers of blue, black, and violet. In the hours when wolves roamed free, I was the hungriest predator, with a sharp gaze, cold and yet boiling blood, no fear and a heart swollen with every kind of evil. Insomniacs are incongruous, mentally-ill heroes, who watch over everything without asking anything in return for themselves. They only wonder how far they are into the night. If they closed their eyes, the whole world would suffer. They toss and turn, pressed by the responsibility of keeping watch in the silence and the lone and unachievable desire for a grave-like sleep that erases everything, starting with themselves.

I wasn't sleeping and therefore wasn't dreaming, but I hallucinated as had happened to me in the past. My wish was granted: Pino came to me. Leaning against the doorframe, arms crossed, chewing on a wheat stalk, he smiled crookedly. Hey, you little beast, he said faintly. I suddenly snapped out of it, ashamed of the state in which my brother had found me. We looked at each other for a long time; I hadn't been this happy since the last day we were together.

"You have to come home, Luci'. We have to go for a swim," he ordered, as serious as I'd ever seen him. "Then we'll sleep on the warm earth of the *Muntagna*,"[16] I said, unsure whether it was a statement or a question.

"Okay, Luci'. Do you know how to keep a secret?"

"Yes." I smiled.

"Good girl. Now sleep."

Pino had come to bring me home. My brother was saving me. I always did what he told me to do, and I was finally able to fall asleep.

---

16   Literally "the Mountain"; here meaning Mount Etna.

*

Before I left I had to take care of everything. There had never been much in the house; all I had to do was clean it thoroughly of my pain in order to make it look new and empty, ready to be finally furnished as if it had never been lived in. I covered the furniture with heavy white sheets, took the mirror off the wall and placed it face down. I aired the house out for two days and nights, freezing, convinced that I couldn't get sick since Pino had asked me to leave. The cold altered my mind without the need for liquids or smoke, to which I'd never developed an addiction anyway. They were means to suffer, which I chose to use with scientific care and accuracy. There is pleasure in hurting oneself, mainly when one can tell someone else that it was their fault. Then I closed and locked the windows and shutters, so whoever came after me would find a musty odor. I had to leave a small warning, a sign of what had happened, the outline of a corpse that had been taken away.

We had never truly owned that house, rented for years at a certain rate per month. The butcher saw it as a burden and a sure sign of failure. I realized at that moment how grateful I was for the sense of lightness that came from not putting down roots. Closing everything up, wedging a piece of life in there and not worrying about it anymore. Abandoning and forgetting an ungrateful, unappreciative place that had refused to be filled. Slipping off my wedding ring and placing it on the kitchen table, turning off the lights.

I resigned from my job. I wouldn't miss the phones, they multiplied the voices I heard in my head. Maybe the long apron we used in the office would be the only thing I'd regret; it had helped me blend in with the others. It was humble and simple, like the place I came from, letting us comfort ourselves with the reassuring belief that we were all the same.

I'd written down in my notebook the stories I didn't want to forget. Sometimes you say the most wonderful things in a whisper, right before trampling them with other words. Those who had spoken and those who had listened to those words might forget them, but I wouldn't. I wonder what would have become of me if I had stopped writing. My notebook had become many notebooks, where I wound the thick skein of life, my truth. In the end, a good memory and a sharp pen are the only things I've truly possessed.

I hadn't saved much, but I had enough to pay for my trip and to get by for a couple of months. I knew however that in my hometown people are simultaneously alive and dead. The main trait developed there was the tendency to survive. Limbs made dry in the sun, we never had anything, yet we didn't die, always weak but resilient. A new and genuine surprise accompanied the end of each of us, when we couldn't go on any longer and gave up and let ourselves die. It was as if we didn't really need to eat or drink, to cover ourselves or to rest; we were pieces of mud and earth, content without sorrow simply because we didn't know anything better. Our time was the daylight, the stars at night, boredom during the day, and we were always waiting. Sweaty and tired.

I prepared my things, which, like the butcher's, were quickly gathered. I lovingly dusted off my cardboard suitcase, the one that had accompanied me up North and was now bringing me back home. The cold and time had cracked it in several places, but I hoped it would withstand the last journey I was asking it to take with me. Lastly, I sat at the table, paper and pen in hand, to explain to Catena that I would never return. That's when I realized that I'd always written, but never spoken to anyone. *Dear Catena…* and then the emptiness and the fear of what I might have said. I'd have liked to bring her back with me, but I knew she believed in America and was content and satisfied there, where she was not happy. I couldn't resign myself to not belonging anywhere; I felt out of place.

I only wrote that I had no choice but to run away, to escape, even without a proper goodbye. I was aware of my despicable act, leaving her alone, and discovered within me a nearly unbearable lightheartedness. I put together sloppy, appalling words that I didn't want to think, but that explained myself well: if I'd had a child, I would have abandoned him too, I would have left him there.

It wasn't necessary, but I folded the sheet and placed it in an envelope. As I licked the bitter glue on the edge, I thought of my wedding day. We had chosen a civil ceremony. Luckily Anna and my father were already dead; our decision would have made one roll her eyes and sent the other to bed for a few days. The butcher and I shared the unpleasant feeling of being watched every time we entered a church, which is why neither of us had set foot in one for years, something we didn't talk much about. It was a disappointment to Catena, who still decided to gift me my shoes and dress. Catena taught me the ways of adulthood and was anxious that I always confront it with the right clothes. We chose a white dress, cinched at the waist and with a gauzy skirt that fell halfway to my dark calves. A lace bolero covered my chest and shoulders, leaving my forearms and delicate wrists bare. The neckline was scandalously exposed, and we'd chosen a daring pair of pointed ivory shoes with a slight heel. A veil would have been too much, but I had blue and azure flowers intertwined in my braided hair, along with a bouquet of scentless white tulips. All that was missing was something old and borrowed. Like my mother years before, once I was dressed Catena drew near to pierce my ears with a pair of small pearl studs. Unlike Anna, however, she was gentle, guiding the pearls through my earlobes to settle in place. A timid drop of blood emerged from one piercing, quickly dabbed away by Catena with a handkerchief before it could stain the dress.

Throughout the day, I shivered from the cold, struggled to breathe properly. I couldn't even enjoy the pearls I had long desired because my earlobes felt like they were on fire, drumming wildly. My heels ached in pain, pierced by a crown of pins. I felt the imposing presence of a thin band of yellow gold around the circumference of my left ring finger. Everyone told me I looked beautiful. The butcher laughed, magnificent in his elegant suit, moving comfortably as though it were made for him.

*

It was the only time in my life that I returned to my Southern hometown, to complete a journey that had begun almost twenty years earlier. I knew the pain wouldn't pass. When pain passes, it's only because life also passes, and the end closes over everything, leaving nothing more to see, hear, smell, or taste.

Nonetheless, I was reclaiming my mind piece by piece, beginning to understand everything, I left to put my bones back together. Above all, I was leaving because Pino had asked me to.

There's nothing that holds more promise than a pretty young girl. I was a promise unfulfilled, a faded *fimmina*. For me, love has never come at the right time. I lit it too soon, with Netto, a flash in the darkness of childhood repaid with my mother's slaps. And then too late, in the wrong place, with a man who couldn't meet me halfway. Loving him had consumed me, aged me. I wasn't old like a mother or a grandmother; I was old without dignity, without respect, like something that no longer works, left to gather dust, a barren land unable to bear fruit.

There was nothing else left for me. Returning to the places I'd come from and that I'd forgotten I belonged to. The prickly pears and blackberries, the white clothes and terraced houses. The stout man sleeping in his fruit truck, the children on the bus screaming and banging their heads together like marbles. The spotted stray cats. My past returned to my mind, as lively and colorful as it had never been, in the shape of a legend I'd let myself be told by people who maybe had never even seen my village, my land. I'd become a foreigner myself, I liked to believe the amusing idiocies that attract the curious.

I was crossing the continent to return home, by land and by sea. A small boat promised the impossible: to reach the island in a handful of hours. That crossing cost me little compared to the journey ahead, which for me turned back time rather than space. A bargain-rate magic, like those of my aunt. It seemed fitting, as I was returning to her as well: it was our way of doing things.

What was actually crazy was that the train that took me to the nearest port cost much more. Was it was worth it, so dumb, capable only of going up and down, forward and back on a track? Identical, rational, linear, whereas for a paltry fee you could expect to cross the water, to skirt around islands, to cut through schools of fish.

I boarded on a twisted, rocky coast, two hours away from the gray city I didn't even turn to say goodbye to. The city of my independence was more arid than the desert where I was born. Elsewhere, perhaps, the butcher would have continued to love me; elsewhere, perhaps, love would have found nourishment. I harbored the fearful suspicion that wherever I went, I'd carry with me a narrow, dead, uninhabitable place. That place was me.

Onboard the train, I chose a compartment that was still empty, awkwardly sliding the glass door as I pushed my suitcase inside with my hips. I'd just settled in, still panting from the effort, irritated by the sudden heat that had flushed my face, when a young woman with a little boy entered. She kicked her suitcase to make it slide across the floor while holding her son in her arms. I watched her without greeting her or offering to help, feeling both satisfied and slightly guilty. She stopped and stared back at me. After a few seconds, she asked if I would hold the child, placing him in my lap without even waiting for an answer. Women often grant each other undeserved trust; I was probably the least suitable person for the task. I stiffened under the child's watchful gaze. The mother lifted her suitcase and placed it in the overhead rack opposite, huffing in exasperation. She collapsed in her seat without taking her son back from me. She gripped the armrests with both hands, eyes closed and face red, blowing away the hair that had stuck to her forehead. Minutes passed as she rested. Then she opened her eyes and looked at me. What's your name, she asked me, and without wanting to lie, I answered what came naturally. Anna. Meanwhile, the little boy had nestled against my flat chest. For a few minutes, I was my mother holding my brother Pino in my arms. Then the young woman thanked me, took him back, hugged him to her, and closed her eyes again as she stroked his hair.

*

The train stopped just before it could plummet. The station faced straight toward the expanse of sky and sea, aiming at the dark line of the horizon. A sign pointed to the port, and many of us headed toward the ships. The woman from my compartment gave me a melancholy smile before heading in the opposite direction, limping under the weight of her luggage. The little boy gripped her hand, twisting his hair around his fingers. In a few seconds, they were far away and lost from sight, and I only had time to realize that I'd felt something for them. I wondered how long I would remember them; I turned around and continued on.

Among the many vessels docked at the port, I managed to find mine, small enough to be frightening. It was stronger than me; I crossed myself, not knowing exactly to whom I was entrusting my safety. I tried to calm myself by remembering that the sea and I had a secret. Approaching the water had always done me good.

I smiled shyly, believing I already felt at home as I walked along the slippery plank that led onto the shabby boat, which was as unsteady as I felt. They seated me on a faux leather chair, broken in several places, in the middle of a row of other chairs and other waiting passengers. Everything would be fine, everything would be fine, everything would be fine. But the sea is alive. I naively believed it was my comrade simply because it had welcomed me when I was a girl. I didn't know the sea at all—the real sea, tall and rough and constantly moaning. My whole body started to shake after barely an hour, tormented by streams of cold sweat. Looking ahead was torture, looking at my feet was agony, and trying to save myself by staring out the porthole was even worse. My stomach twisted up into my throat in a constant wail. My eyes threatened to flee from their sockets; it was hard to think of myself as a whole, with every part of me mutinying. I felt like I was about to dissolve, as if I were held together by a thread suddenly cut by the sea and I, too, was made of waves. I was confused, pluralized.

Seven hours, and it felt like much longer. I vomited my guts out in foul-smelling spurts, my hands gripping a filthy toilet, my heart squeezed by a giant's fist. I cried from the effort, I was exhausted. No one around seemed concerned about my state, which clearly didn't impress the crew members or my fellow passengers. Some were in the same condition; far from being unexpected, it was completely normal. As usual, I was counted among the weak. Wounded by disappointment, I was purged of all evil; in its extremist and violent way, the sea did me a favor.

All in all, lying on the floor, dirty, drenched in sweat, exhausted, I was grateful. It seemed fitting. I admitted to myself that I'd been afraid.

*

In my ears, an insect-like ringing. I disembarked at lunchtime, which in our parts is a disturbingly peaceful sanctuary; anyone who breaks the silence has shattered a precious vase. I found my fellow countrymen reserved, almost secretive, from the first confused exchanges with the people at the port. I'm not sure if I remembered them that way; I had the absurd impression of reaching home and seeing these places for the first time. I was rejected from every direction, not really from the place where I lived, yet no longer belonging to my origins, which had spat me out and now took me back almost with pity, with the suspicion reserved for a dubious wanderer whose origins and intentions are unknown. A man, one of the less distrustful ones, approached me cautiously before stepping back, then finally brought himself to whisper, unasked, "We still have peace here, God willing. It's quiet, and everything is beautiful," just a few words, goodbye, have a nice day. And I knew in my heart that he was lying, as we all lie when we say only good things about the place that made us and turned us into what we are.

I wondered then, and still do, what drives seaside towns to fray around the edges of the port. All the same, their streets radiate from there in every direction, shabby and smelly, soulless. Choosing a path is an act of faith and courage, or else a trap you fall into without realizing it, as if it were a rotten, overly deep well. It's taken for granted that anyone arriving knows where to go, as if they had a ball of thread in their pocket to follow. No signs, just a memory that's supposed to be prepared and well-trained, which mine was not. The village was still far away, and I struggled to find the bus that would finally drop me off in front of my real home. It was early, but the moon was already high in the sky.

Exhausted, my guts twisted and eyes burning, I decided to enter a tavern that had a nice smell. I don't know where I found the wish to eat anything; I couldn't have been hungry. I just wanted to erase the taste of bile that was tormenting my teeth and palate. I sat at a rough table in the far corner, in the company of twins with empty, cataract-veiled eyes. I soon realized that only one of them spoke, though always in the plural and only when necessary. He politely asked if I was all right, what I had ordered, and if I needed utensils, although I was clearly holding them in my right hand. I raised them to show him, he smiled and fell silent, not exchanging another word, neither with me nor with his twin. At the open door, a woman, no longer young but made pretty by a black dress with white flowers, was choking on a hoarse, drunken laugh. Her legs were bare and her arms alluring, and she was overly made-up, making me think that much must have changed. I was surprised by an unexpected pang of envy for a lighthearted life, carried by the warm wind, like her dress. My order arrived just then. Out of spite, I hungrily pounced on a grilled squid. The meal consumed my entire mind, reducing me to the animal that I am. I also remember meeting the gray eyes of a bored girl, who let them wander into the void without listening to what a man, probably hers, was saying to her. She fanned herself with a handkerchief, without moving a bit of air. She was tired, wishing to be anywhere but there with us, who knows where her thoughts were taking her. I was on the verge of asking her to come with me, even opened my mouth, but said nothing and resumed chewing in silence.

After dinner, I decided to spend the night in a small hotel nearby, knowing I wouldn't be able to walk much further. The ground swayed beneath my feet, and I couldn't shake the feeling of being between the waves. Once in bed, I saw the ceiling spinning above my head. Closing my eyes made the rolling sensation even more insistent. Lying on the water, I thought about a pair of gray eyes and their failed salvation.

*

The bus dropped me off in the dust. I arrived in the village on All Souls' Day, a still-warm November afternoon. I dragged the loving weight of my dead on my shoulders. The street smelled good, with *ossa di morto*[17] baking in the ovens and on the street vendors' stalls, giving off an inviting aroma, though they threatened to break your

---

17   Literally "Bones of the Dead", traditional Sicilian crunchy almond cookies shaped like skulls and baked to celebrate All Souls' Day.

teeth. It was a true holiday; old men and women from the past brought children toys and let themselves be nibbled on without really being scary. My fellow villagers have never been afraid of death. A tight band around my head pressed so hard on my temples that I almost didn't feel pain anymore. For a moment, I believed I'd become a saint, dead among the dead.

Only twelve hundred remained, a few, the worst. My aunt among them, and later I discovered that Netto had also stayed. The village had a few more buildings, the ones I had seen as a child being built brick by brick toward the sky, which—which I'd never seen—were old by now, abandoned, and needed to be rebuilt. My village has always been dying.

I felt a deep stab of happiness between my ribs because the light was warm and alive. Then, nothing more. I walked slowly along the path leading to the stone house where I'd grown up. The road seemed short and the house small, so much so that I wondered if I'd taken the wrong direction. One thing remained unchanged: no one had built anything on the road leading up to it.

I stopped a few feet from the dark wooden door, open wide to let the rooms breathe. My aunt, dressed in black, was sitting on a straw chair and weaving a wicker basket. She looked up. I felt like I hadn't lived my life at all, as if we had just said farewell a moment before. Nothing that wasn't the South had ever existed. Nothing had happened; I was waking up now, back to my raw, perhaps cruel, sunbaked life. Luci', said my aunt, acknowledging my presence. And then, simply, *trase*, come in. And I followed her, like a moth to a flame, happy that just the two of us had survived, alone.

I hadn't let her know I was coming, yet it was as if she had been expecting me. What a lovely gift *me puttanu i motti noshri*,[18] she said with a smile. I confirmed it, explaining that it was Pino who had dragged me back there; my aunt always knew everything there was to know. She gently motioned for me to sit down. We sat at the table and spent a few seconds looking at each other in silence. *Cosa mi*

---

18 "Our dead have brought me."

cunti?,[19] she asked and, needing to sum up twenty years all at once, all I could answer was *nenti.*[20] I didn't know how to quickly regain the habit that builds daily life.

My aunt got up and brought a loaf of fresh bread and a plate full of white grapes to the table. Then she filled a pitcher with ice-cold water and handed me a frosted glass. We remained silent. After a few minutes, she got up again to place some cookies on an embroidered napkin, *ossa di morto* and sesame-seed *reginelle.*[21] There was a fly overturned on the windowsill, its legs stiff in the air. It was lost, maybe it had been banging against a glass pane for hours. Its pointless death moved me deeply.

In the beginning, my aunt didn't say much except *mancia mancia.*[22] Grapes and bread should be eaten together, and as I began to chew, my thoughts turned to Catena.

Then she mentioned Anna's name, and then immediately after my father's and Pino's, recalling them in detail as if she wanted to paint a family portrait. She described my mother's last days, how she seemed grateful for her confused condition, freed from her burdens. She had left this earth lighter than a breath of air. With a sigh, my aunt mimed my mother dying.

Not knowing how to respond, I lied: thinking back to the journey of the previous day, I told her I had dreamed that night of rough seas and a devilish wind blowing. She replied, satisfied and cryptic, almost witchlike, that dreams make reality and rough seas bring cats out of their holes. *Ora dogu ci vole, magari u miu uscirà fora.*[23]

As we talked, my aunt nibbled on hard bread that she pulled occasionally out of her apron pocket. I'm not hungry, she said, but I feel a hole here that needs filling, pointing to her thin, shriveled stomach. I've lost my appetite, and she chewed, slowly and tirelessly.

---

19   "What's new?"

20   "Nothing."

21   Traditional Sicilian cookies, round and crumbly.

22   "Eat up."

23   "By the way, mine might come out too."

My people have a dual, obsessive relationship with food: we think about it constantly. Claiming disinterest, we despise food while cooking and eating it. It's only just good enough and you swallow it to survive, bread accompanies the meal because otherwise it's a sin. But if a guest, like I was, crosses the threshold, there's no other way to welcome them. Food must suffocate them, pursue them, fill them to exhaustion, so as to cloud their vision and take away their desire to speak. You constantly goad them, *mancia mancia*, and the encouragement turns perilously into a threat. You blackmail them with the risk of offense, not caring if they don't feel like it, if it might make them sick.

I told her briefly about my marriage, with few details, I didn't want her to imagine that we'd been happy. I wanted her to know I hadn't abandoned the future she had given me. Among *fimmine*, we would have done things properly. He, on the other hand, had forgotten, he hadn't had the strength to resist.

"*Ca ciettu,*[24] God wasn't watching over you," said my aunt, as if I'd lost sight of the point. I had trusted a man's promise, but what you should never believe a lover's word.

"*U Signuruzzu a chistu serve,*[25] to make sure the promise is kept." And then, seeing the retort forming on my lips, she added: "By both sides." I thought that when you don't believe in God at a time and in a place you should, others find ways to make sure you start.

Perhaps my aunt saw me grow pale, because she rushed to comfort me. She touched her chest with her index finger, *un puntu buio ca avi a aviri.*[26] She wished him the deepest regret for his whole life, so deep he'd never be able to lift his head again.

"*Avrà chiddu ca merita. Acqua davante, ventu d'arrere e saponata ne pere: aspettamu ca sciddica.*"[27] She cursed him almost affectionately.

She told me with joy about her solitary years, how sometimes thoughts get stuck in the weave of baskets. Our house had stood still

---

24 "Of course."

25 "That's what the Lord is for." *U Signuruzzu* is an affectionate term.

26 "He must have darkness in here."

27 "He'll get what he deserves. Water before him, wind behind him and soapsuds at his feet: just wait for him to slip."

in time, but the village had moved forward, not necessarily for the better. She mentioned a few names, told me stories of families whose memory hadn't taken root in me. They were empty voices racing around the room, passing through us unheard.

At last I found the courage to ask about Netto, pronouncing his name softly. My aunt lit up for a moment and said, with a good-natured laugh, that it was harder to forget the only child of the sun we'd ever had in the village. But then she abruptly added that before saying anything else, it was better for me to know that Netto was dead. Disappointment and surprise hit me like a fury, I remained silent because I had no other choice. My aunt came near as if to extend a hand and reassure me, but then she withdrew without touching me. Netto wasn't the boy I'd known when we were children. We both realized that, despite the pain of learning about his death, he was a man I'd never truly known. My Netto had died the day I took the train. I listened to what followed, holding my breath, almost expecting a different ending than the one I'd been told. I waited in vain for an alternative conclusion to the one the story had begun with.

With a smile that made him friends with the world, Netto, at a very young age had developed two wrinkles on his face, on each side, vertically, up to the corners of his eyes. My aunt touched her cheeks with her thumbs, to show me exactly where. He had grown tall, almost tall enough to reach the stars; thanks to his dark skin and hair, he looked like he came straight from the depths of the earth. The boy had studied as much as was allowed in our village, showing a particular aptitude for numbers. His quicksilver tongue and talent for persuasion, combined with restrained ambition, made him a perfect salesman. That's how, after a series of small jobs, he was hired to sell sewing machines in our village and the nearby towns. And that's also how he met Melina, the young seamstress from a village not far from ours. Melina had silky blonde hair, well-kept nails and a bird brain. She answered the door and was soon persuaded to let him in, to make him coffee, to allow him to court her. By the end of the day, Netto had sold one of his machines and met his future wife.

Melina was pretty, but not overly so, a seamstress with no talent, inelegant but with many demands, who aped a foreign dialect to feel important. Above all, Melina wasn't a *fimmina* to fool around with, because she was the daughter of Netto's uncle, a step-brother of his father's who ensured things were settled as needed. It wasn't a hardship for Netto; he was inclined toward love and fell in love, even with someone who didn't deserve him. She, on the other hand, married him for his *piccioli*, but soon showed no interest in the marriage as a union or partnership. When they went to bed at night, she promptly turned her back on him. *Cose ri mali cristiani*,[28] no child ever came from their union. Inevitable; I thought of myself and the butcher, of the salt on our roots.

Melina was the complete opposite of Netto. Devoted to her elderly mother, unpopular with people, and with no friends, she quit working as soon as she had the chance to indulge daily in what little she had, solely for herself. Netto had learned to survive in the desert since childhood, enjoying a reserve of lightheartedness that seemed inexhaustible. But growing up in a slowly disappearing village, tied to an airheaded woman, engaged in a job that promised fortune but never delivered, even Netto had stopped shining. Perhaps because he'd once been known for his cheerfulness, his wasted intelligence had become the silent symbol of disaster. *Malacumminatu*, people said, torn between sorrow for the slow agony of a special man and relief to see him put back in his place, an unfulfilled destiny like all the rest. Netto ended up spending most of his time alone, in a bachelor's house, as dirty as if he'd never taken a wife. Melina always had *chiffari*, *s'a viri idda picchi n'avissi sempre a ghiri ne so matri*.[29] She spent very little time with Netto, liking best to criticize him from a distance; she could hardly stand his company. His solitude, that was the key. One evening, Netto lit a cigarette and lay down in bed where he fell asleep while smoking, *botta ri veleno, catenacci nu coddu*.[30] No one can say whether he did so on purpose or not. It was a holocaust. They found him the next day, consumed by the flames.

---

28 "Unchristian deeds," also used to mean "unbelievable."

29 "… something to do, only she knows why she always had to go to her mother's house."

30 Shot of poison, chains around the neck, used here to mean "Damn it!"

Along with other women from the village, my aunt was tasked with washing the stained shape from the floor, cleaning the house, and setting it in order for mourning; you couldn't expect a widow to carry out such a wearisome task.

Throughout the funeral, the church filled with the undignified cries of Melina, who loudly shrieked *facennu schifiu* Netto's name as though it were an obscene word. My aunt told me that in that moment, she'd hoped that we don't return after death, because Netto didn't deserve to witness a disaster that made people's hair stand on end.

With her husband's death, Melina found the role for which she was born, a wronged widow basking in the loving memory of a man who'd kicked the bucket when it was time to be on his way. She'd been sacrificed, but now the time had come to enjoy the only thing she'd truly craved: being alone. Melina had been right about one thing: a widow isn't a spinster. She was safe now.

Mischino.[31]

Then my aunt fell silent. A few moments later, I asked where he was buried, I'd go visit him the following day. She briskly explained how to find the grave, then started talking again, but I was no longer listening.

Netto had been the only child of the sun, thriving under its warmth. All around was dead countryside.

*

The profound impact hearing about his death had on me corroborated what I'd always known and refused to admit, even to myself. I had never forgotten him. When an encounter burns you, even after years, even if nothing happened, you remember it with the steadfastness of hot embers in the fireplace that burn all night and keep smoldering until dawn. Netto had never been absent from me because he'd always been with me. I didn't understand how I hadn't felt his death.

I got up and told my aunt I'd be back before dark. I needed to walk, to go toward the sea. I remembered that the road leading to

---

31 "Poor man."

the beach stretched a few miles away toward a small rocky hill that plunged down to the water. On the outermost edge, when I was a child, there was a square-shaped cottage carved into the rock, an ancient watchtower. I wanted to check if it was still there. I crossed a dense olive grove, interrupted here and there by patches of prickly pear cacti. The path was damp and white, dotted with sharp stones that wounded me through my shoes. I could hear echoes of mine and Pino's shouts, from when we would mercilessly drop rocks onto the helpless bodies of small, scaly living things. I spotted the tower as I reached the highest point. I descended toward it, following a makeshift staircase hammered into the hill. I sat down in front of the entrance, on the last of the three steps leading to the door. I closed my eyes for a moment, trying to capture the scent of wild fennel. Then I looked down toward a small natural pool. The water must have been warm.

As though it were an act of courage, I sank hesitantly toward the ground. I slowly lay down on the soil mixed with sand, gazing up at the sky. Netto was beside me, now an adult. I saw a face with intriguing asymmetries, curly black hair and weather-beaten skin. I pictured him more reserved and taciturn than when he was a child, capable of making sarcastic remarks about me, then grinning with the same wild laughter that I knew well and that unsettled me to my very core. If we'd grown up together, we'd have loved each other until out love turned to hate, like everyone who gets married—especially in my village. It had happened to me, too. I would have found myself living beside a petty man who'd once been a lively boy whose brilliance had died out. Like everyone else, he felt like he was different and would initially have been proud to have married a *fimmina curiusa*,[32] who wants, desires, and labors like *nu masculo*. But then who knows how many times he'd have been so tired tired tired tired of listening to me, though maybe not enough to raise his hand against me, against our things. He would have cursed his rash choice every day. I know the reasons he was attracted to me would have become his greatest torment. I wasn't like Melina, and he'd have been unhappy all the same. I wanted to dream of him as a real man, with all men's bad thoughts,

32 *"Curiusa"* can mean curious or odd, strange.

bad actions, acid, and bile. I wanted to picture him the way I felt. I allowed myself however the luxury of thinking of him as loyal, that he would always have chosen to lie beside me. I smiled at the thought that this was how the greatest revenge was carried out, soiled with damp sand: to prefer as a companion a sloppy boy who'd once kissed my ears over a legal, official husband of sixteen years. I thanked the butcher for teaching me about the cinema. A lesson I'd taken to heart.

I got up suddenly and composed myself. I shook the dust off from my dress and smoothed it with open palms. I continued down to the beach, undressed, and began to make my way to the water. The pool was as warm as I'd imagined. I approached the rocky barrier separating me from the open sea, the real one. I climbed it, my eyes blurred from the salt, and stood for a while watching the water without really fixing my gaze on any specific point, balancing precariously on the rocks. I felt the skin prickle on my arms and thighs, the already dry fold of my armpits. I dove beyond the stone wall, immersing myself again, this time in thick, cold milk. Finally at peace.

I remained horizontal on the surface of the water, occasionally a wave made me drink some of it and I shook with an irritable cough. Hours might have passed, I decided to turn back when I felt the sea change its mood, swelling until it swallowed the rocks and the path back to the pool. I had to swim for a few yards, the current had carried me far out. I climbed with a fervor I didn't know I possessed, scratching my hands and knees, which began to bleed painlessly. The salt healed the wounds in an instant. Once I reached the beach, I dressed with unnatural slowness, paying attention to every single movement. The dry clothes stuck to my damp skin in an instant, warming me pleasantly. I leaned my head forward, wrung the water out of my hair, then tousled it with my fingers to give it some body. Despite it being fall, I must have gotten some color; I felt it before I could even see it, the tip of my nose tingling.

While I was heading back, a few wild bats and the last mosquitoes of the season flew around me. My hair dried slowly, curly and stiff with salt. The road back seemed endless, maybe because I was surprised by a violent storm when I still had a long way to go. Terrified by the thunder and lightning, I began to run with my hands over my ears and elbows around my head, protecting myself. When I reached the threshold of my house, I knocked like a fugitive in need of shelter. My aunt opened the door but didn't let me in immediately. She stared at me while I shook with fright. *A frevi ti facisti venire, bestia.*[33]

Two days later, when the weather cleared and I was no longer shaking, I went in search of Netto's grave. I told him about the sea, as he had done to me. I wasn't wearing earrings and bent down to kiss the tombstone.

*

You're always hungry, the letter said. It had taken her some time to understand, perhaps to forgive, but Catena had finally replied. You're always hungry, and you've always been hungry, and those who hunger are alive.

Two things about Catena struck me: her ability to highlight the truth hidden in plain sight, and her ability to see through me. She was like everything rooted in the body, like teeth, the tangle of guts, nerves, and veins.

Her words reached me in a state of suspension. I acted as if something was yet to come, as if my entire life still lay ahead of me. Just like when I was an incomplete girl, helping my aunt with household chores so she could go into town to sell her baskets, read fortunes, ward off the evil eye and cast spells, trying to procure what little we could put in our mouths. I made it down to the sea almost every day, hoping to lose myself there. Sometimes I slashed the air with a stick or, bored, uprooted some dry plants in the fields. I spent my days getting dirty with salt or mud, walking just inches from the ground, never achieving complete peace. I held my breath and constantly suffered a hiccup in my stomach, like when you accidentally skip a step and fear falling before you manage to put your hands forward. I didn't know if I was young or old, I couldn't understand the origins and direction of the desire simmering low inside of me.

Sometimes I'd stop at the bar in the square, run by old Liborio,

---

33   "You've made yourself sick, foolish girl."

whose white hair and blue eyes didn't entirely convince me of his kindness. It was well known that he was involved in a lot of goings on. I wasn't exactly sure what that meant; it certainly didn't involve the *barchette alle visciole*,[34] pistachio cones, ricotta and chocolate cakes, jam twists or donuts displayed in the counter, but no one talked about it, and I didn't ask any questions. I limited myself to drinking and eating, just to keep my mouth busy. Even if I had wanted to, I couldn't have chosen another place; Liborio was the only one in town who baked *duci*.

He may not have been as good as the things he baked, yet he proved interesting right from the start. I appreciated him reluctantly and he, just as reluctantly, wanted to know all about me. No one was surprised I'd run away: I was the crazy woman's daughter, the witch's niece, and had lost the protection of every man in the family. It was incredible that I was back again, that there was something worse, a bigger failure, somewhere out here. Mine was a miraculous and worrying presence, like an apparition. I was the one who had returned, screwing myself onto a twisted destiny with the stubbornness of a goat butting its head against the fence.

When someone entered the bar, by an unspoken agreement, both Liborio and I stopped talking, jealous of the secrets we shared.

Our conversations, made up of few words, began to pay my bill. My dry reports of America were worth as much to Liborio as hard cash. I thought back to Catena and when she would force me to talk about the luxury of houses she'd never live in. As uninterested as she had been in the pain I'd felt, Liborio wanted more and more.

His wife would often come by to ask me if I wanted more coffee, driving her husband crazy.

"You don't offer coffee; you just pour it," he'd repeat with increasing annoyance.

If the donuts were still warm, he'd ask if I wanted some. They're special, made fresh, *uora uora*. I learned from Liborio's outbursts that "do you want" is only asked of the sick, and soon enough a couple would appear on a small plate in front of me. Then I'd go back to

---

34   Boat-shaped cakes filled with *visciole*, small, bitter cherries.

answering questions while the sugar burned my fingers.

I told Catena about the sea, the fields, my conversations with Liborio, mainly made up of silence, where both of us, sitting on chairs outside the door, let time pass as we stared ahead. At the end of his gaze, surely, America.

I asked her to join me, to testify to my affection, knowing full well she never would. I said and asked nothing about the butcher. My letters probably spoke of him even when I didn't mention him at all.

I tried to tell her what it meant to be young again at my age. As a child, I'd grown up prematurely, a mother to my mother and to myself. Now I was a grownup child, cheeky and without a shadow of responsibility, capable of understanding what should or shouldn't be said and doing whatever I wanted. I liked to torment clods of earth in front of the door of the house, to make the heart beat. Then I had to scrub my nails thoroughly under a jet of cold water, but at least I could experience pleasure. She, like perhaps all women, would understand: we're always, right from the start, young and old, new and eternal, at the same time.

Returning to the village meant lost time and dense thoughts. I tried to describe the changes that had occurred; for once, I knew more than she did.

*

My aunt only spoke to me when we sat down to eat, as if food loosened her tongue. The rest of the time, she allowed herself to be observed. I admired her while she wove her baskets, I stared at her while she sewed, hypnotized by her skillful hands. Cooking together was out of the question. Preparing meals was her domain; I enjoyed watching her bend over clouds of steam, engrossed in stirring eggs dancing in a pot.

We woke up together at dawn to enjoy the only cool hour available, and even before our day started, we fluffed our pillows and straightened our rooms. In silence. My aunt heated water and let a slice of lemon steep in it, a proved way to cause evacuation. She drank it standing on the doorstep, letting the cat, which had meanwhile returned, stroke her legs with its upright, cheerful tail. In silence. We got used to each other's presence, impatiently sipping diluted black coffee and biting into bread spread with orange honey. She addressed me starting with practical matters. "Is there any bread?" she'd ask as she sat down, knowing full well that we'd never been without bread since the war ended. At breakfast, she let herself be served, allowing me to cut my slices and hers, to spread the honey, to pour the coffee. In return, she'd tell me about her dreams, her memories and prophecies. I dreamed little or nothing, my eyes open or shut; my job was to listen, to listen to her.

Then our paths would diverge until evening, and it was still silence and solitude. It fell to me to empty the water onto the floors, to bend down and sweep, to wash the sheets and hang them on a line strung without much conviction between two poles planted in the dry grass. Below, the sea, the fields, Liborio, and over everything, anticipation and heat. My hands in the soil, brushing my nails, mid-afternoon cicadas, mosquitoes at night.

And again, dawn, pillows, hot water, the cat, coffee, bread and honey, dreams, memories, and prophecies, a bucket of water on the floor, rectangles of white cloth in the sun, the sea, the fields, Liborio. My hands in the soil, brushing my nails, mid-afternoon cicadas, mosquitoes at night.

And again.

*

The butcher's shop in the village had recently been left without an owner. He'd been young and athletic, as strong as the bulls he led to slaughter. When we least expected it, the night struck him with an apoplectic blow, depriving him of a future and the town of its meat.

Thus, the dragging cycle of my days was interrupted with a precise blow of the axe. It so happened that my marriage finally proved useful to me, for reasons I hadn't foreseen. Marriage had actually been a school, and my husband a teacher; he'd made me the queen of the butcher's shop and unwittingly provided me with a job. Thanks to him, I had become refined enough to serve customers, but I knew how to be stern and determined in the workshop, accustomed to the cold of light, metal, and air.

I still wonder who watched over me, ensuring the right thing, a profession I knew, independence, a salvific escape from the strict circle my life had become. I never asked if they found salt in the home of the prematurely and suddenly deceased young man, so as not to think him murdered and not to have to give a name to my suspicions. I stepped forward as his replacement.

My proposal was initially met with reluctance, almost disgust. They accepted out of necessity, but there was something perverse about a *schetta*[35] wanting to plunge her hands into steaming entrails. Butchery isn't women's work. Women wring chickens' necks in the countryside, slit pigs' throats; they don't manage a shop alone where animals are gutted from the inside. They don't know how to dissect, treat, preserve, or trade animals. A woman of attractive appearance doesn't go well with a bloodstained apron. My solitude was the subject of criticism and *cuttigghiu*.[36] But the novelty soon lost its appeal, as is often the case. If something doesn't always work, it doesn't mean it never should: the best way to subvert a law is to do things differently. People aren't so attached to norms; in life, there are more urgent things than tradition. They were surprised by my resilience and, without even realizing it, some people—a few at first, but then more frequently, began to admire me. I had the impression that, ultimately, everyone who remained was a broken promise. Those who had left had at least managed to escape; all the others had was the village. Survivors are pragmatic people; they just need you to know how to do your job. Moreover, *masculo* and *fimmina* weren't the same as when I left; both had fallen apart, *nuddo*[37] was *nenti* anymore.

I was strange. Up North, I hadn't been a lady, but I knew how to conceal my origins behind polite manners. My accent stood out strongly in America; here, it seemed watered down, my tongue moving smoother than the others'. Knives and blood earned me a name. I was the saint of knives, the devoted protector of the ignorant. Friend to a few and always the wrong ones, now daughter only of the heat,

---

35 Young and/or unmarried woman, spinster.

36 Gossip.

37 Nobody.

I inspired a certain fear and a strange form of respect. I was a ghost to the others, who couldn't imagine my beginning and thus my end. The exceptions were Catena, who was far away, Liborio, and my aunt, who were familiar with the flesh I was made of and not the meat I sold in the shop.

I had no *scantu*[38] of killing, but I no longer felt the pleasure I once shared with Pino in squeezing stones between my fingers. Animals cry out when you kill them; you have to be merciful and quick. Most of the time, however, the beasts were already dead when they arrived, the breeders sparing me the trouble. I don't know if this was out of a sense of delicacy and respect or to deprive me of a pleasure they believed only knotted, muscular strength could earn. I didn't want to raise my own animals. It felt unnatural to bring them into the world, raise them, and then take away everything I had given them in a single blow.

Pig ears and rooster combs, tripe, *stigghiola*,[39] tails, tongues, lambs, some rabbits, ribs, quarters, and steaks. Butchers were a modern invention, imported from the city. When I was a child, those who had livestock in the countryside would eat meat only on religious holidays. Calluses, cartilage for frying, the *cosi rintra*,[40] leftovers for ground meat and sausages and poor man's delicacies remained the most sought-after products in my shop. Liver and spleen are my favorites because they require trust from those who eat them. They're black and rich in iron, that's where all the flavor is. If you avoid them, you aren't really eating meat.

I'm like pigs: nothing goes to waste. I had a new opportunity in my hands, and this time I was doing everything alone, relying only on myself. I'd come to understand one thing: since God hadn't been able to be with me always or everywhere (perhaps because I didn't believe in Him) I needed to start depending on myself.

---

38   Fear.

39   Typical Sicilian dish made with entrails.

40   Inner parts (also figuratively).

*

I wrote to Catena regularly. I'd found a way to let someone read the cursed words that had brought me nothing but trouble as a child. Catena was an avid reader. Just as she'd eagerly listened to the stories I told, she now seemed to depend on my written words, answering quickly and enthusiastically. Almost as if we were still sitting at her table, she didn't get lost in details but asked me sparse, direct questions. To make her happy, I'd write down my movements, trying to explain the thoughts that flared up in my mind at the sight of dust in the corners, lemon peels, my aunt's profile—everything that inhabits solitude. I wanted to bring her back to the island without her having to take the train. I told her that the young butcher in town *s'assintu mau* and that the meat business had become mine. It wasn't the first time a death had been convenient for me.

To cover the distance between home and work, I used the bicycle that had marked the beginning of my friendship with Pino. Liborio helped me get it back in shape. The brakes and wheels needed replacing, but when I finished cleaning it, I felt the same thrill as the day we cheated to win it. Straddling melancholy, I adopted a fragile pace, thinking about Pino was so painful.

They say you never forget how to ride a bicycle. With the same ease, I regained my skill with knives. Cutting things up was an exercise in patience; dissecting was a test of logic. Face to face with tissues, muscles, and fat, immersed in their sweetish smell, I could be honest. I searched for fate like a soothsayer with entrails, plunging my hands in up to the wrists. Meat was my protection, my only future.

I brought meat home from time to time, but we mostly ate it just to keep it from spoiling. My aunt had a hard time consuming such rich food, saying she didn't need it. Seventy years, maybe more, spent on bread, milk, and eggs had dictated the taste to her old tongue which, in the end, didn't appreciate what it had long been unable to afford. My aunt had built pleasure on the pattern of habit, her skills in the image and likeness of need. Even if she'd wanted to, she wouldn't have known how to cook meat, except for the poor, dry kind from chickens that had, like us, pecked at the country soil.

I remembered Anna and her constant, yet constantly censored, hunger. She would definitely have found an excuse, or at least a trick, to devour everything, destroying the proof by digestion.

*

One day, Liborio introduced me to a young girl, dragging her to our table as if she were an inert, annoyingly heavy object. Marta had the legendary look of a dark little Madonna, with black, cunning, spiteful eyes and hair tangled like a thicket of prayers. This little animal needed someone to teach her Italian, a rare commodity in our parts. Like everyone else, Liborio cursed, argued, thought, and dreamed in dialect, not even in his silence—even less in his silence—did he leave room for an educated language. The village was now made up almost exclusively of old people; seventy or a hundred years old, it made no difference. You could count on one hand my peers who hadn't chosen to flee or to wither and die prematurely. You didn't even need a hand to count the new ones, the children, white flies standing out against a dark background. There was no school anymore, as it wouldn't have served any purpose.

Marta took the bus to go learn. It was clear to me that this is how our village would end. Marta was a child of the village, belonging to everyone and to no one, and she'd already understood that youth didn't exist here, perhaps it never had. We kicked youth out, locking the door behind it. Go and make someone of yourself, something at least; do it for us.

I was the only one who'd lived an educated life, cultivated enough to bear fruit, the only one who'd come back. Though I dissected life in my shop, like a diligent craftswoman I used words to build life. I used a plain, clear language, simple enough for everyone to understand. I'd always done so. I thought about the conciseness of my collection of words and the reports I'd been producing for Catena for years. I realized that I'd never known how to invent stories. Ever since I was a child, I'd written the way my mother had taught me to live: with only the essentials.

If Marta needed to learn Italian, then that's where we'd start.

With writing. There's no better way to know a language than by constantly taking it apart and putting it back together. There's no better way to understand a place than by writing about it, confiding in paper. A written page should resemble a bare house, where every object is necessary and there's no room for the superfluous, because even empty space holds its own importance. I thought of Anna and our necessarily unadorned rooms.

For Liborio, Italian was just grammar, and that's what he asked me to teach the girl. I could have limited myself to that. But this is the only way I knew how to write, to express *le cosi rintra*. The truth lives and shines on the page and on the plate, in giblets, in the stomach, in the spleen, in the liver, which belong to everyone.

We met at Liborio's table, rarely at first, then more and more often during the empty afternoons. I postponed opening the shop, letting the lunch break stretch until it unraveled. Marta was learning to write, and I was learning to write together with others.

I taught her patience. I'd place a glass in the center of the table and ask her to describe it. I forced her to find the right words, torturing her with synonyms. We wouldn't get up until she'd said everything there was to say, describing it as if we weren't there. I wanted her to describe our surroundings so I could see them with my eyes closed, but I only allowed her a handful of words, so she wouldn't be tempted by the futile pleasure of decoration. You must exert brute force with language, acting both rough and gentle. Handling knives and writing both have things in common with poetry.

Sometimes I'd ask her to tell me about a single word, to choose one that could build a story on its own. I realized that I was teaching her my tricks for expressing exactly what I felt but that you can never truly teach someone to write if they don't already love doing it. Marta might not have known Italian when she came to me, but she was already a writer. She'd look around alertly, knowing she'd be called on to report everything; she was interested in understanding. Though I was the teacher, it was she who made me practice, shifting the way I looked at objects, the appearance of Liborio, the taste and flavor of sweets and coffee. Marta made everything bitter, pleasantly linked with pain.

I strained my muscles as I pedaled, starting to push hard when they were still cold, stretching painfully and with difficulty. After the household chores, my spirit cleansed like the sheets and floors, I spent the morning in the shop, dirtying it with blood again. I ate my plentiful lunch alone, behind the metal shutter, a show always ready to start, hidden in purple backstage. Like Anna, I didn't like to be watched while chewed food traveled down my throat and descended into the depths of a well. I left a space between the shutter and the floor to let in some air and to spy on the feet of passersby, the very few who braved the scorching midday sun, merciless even in winter.

I washed and dried my plate before putting it away with the other dishes I cooked with in the workshop. I slipped out, bending down until I could almost reach and kiss the floor. In my haste, I sometimes scratched my knees on the asphalt. I went to Liborio's, where I sat at a small table, slowly sipping hot coffee, accompanied by a still-warm pastry from the oven and his strange company, dense and taciturn like an islander. I waited for Marta to arrive so we could write together. To pass the time, I scratched off the dried blood scabs with my nail, relieving the itchy and burning feeling.

Marta needed to learn to write about the land, the sea and the wheat, to describe what was happening in our parts. Liborio's table soon became cramped for us. I also had the impression that Marta petitioned for us to be alone. The time I granted her was short; she didn't want to share it with others or to taint it with vulgar sounds. After lunch, before reopening the shop, we spent time together in absorption, digesting and reasoning amid spots of color, which she described as stretches of black, blue, and green, gold sheets. Marta chewed on wheat stalks as Pino had, and I lay beside her, occasionally pulling myself up with elbows firmly planted at right angles. I listened to the pen tip scratch the paper following the rhythm of her thoughts, then asked her to read aloud. I was enchanted by her sharp, clear mind. While she was absorbed in her exercises, I was fascinated by the absence of her curves, her long, thin legs, protruding ribs, the ripe color of her hair, her knotted fingers. She couldn't have been more than fifteen. She took my hand in the suspended hours of the fields, and I let her.

I returned to my shop with a racing heart, feeling guilty and happy, like a child entrusted with an important secret. I smiled as I observed the veins of fat and plunged in the knife, overcome by a favorable omen. Hypnotized, I stared at the marbled steaks passing from hand to hand, exiting through the door, leaving me forever.

*

It's a secret, but only to others, that I've always liked those who can turn me into mush. Marta was independent, as if she came from the woods. She ate little to nothing, yet grew strong and was always at ease. She quickly showed me that she didn't need me. If anyone needed someone, it was me. Counting the hours that separated us was torture and pleasure, a lovers' game.

*

Another letter arrived from America. Catena gave me news I certainly wasn't expecting: the butcher had returned to look for me. Truth be told, she wasn't sure it was him. A man had knocked on the door of her apartment while she was out. Catena's husband was at work, the maid had asked for his first and last name and that he leave a message, but he obstinately kept repeating that he needed to speak with her. The maid hadn't let him in, terrified by the impression that the man was actually a ghost, from whom everything—from his flesh to his name—had fled. It could only have been him, the butcher. He kept banging on the door, not accepting the fact that he hadn't found Catena in her place. He had to speak with her urgently, to find out where I was. Where was Lucia, he was looking for Lucia, he wanted Lucia. The maid responded irritably that she didn't know and even if she did, she certainly wouldn't tell a man with no name. He stopped replying, but the maid was sure he stayed a few more minutes longer; she felt his presence behind the door. He was just a presence, a bodiless shadow.

He, wrote Catena, has always been afraid of losing you, and even more afraid of losing himself near you. He's searching for you, hoping not to find you. He sincerely believed I'd never see him again.

The anxiety of his possible return seized me as simultaneously an unexpected blessing and a curse to be avoided. During the day, his face occupied my mind and crowded my thoughts, along with his hands and his eyes. His teeth.

I realized that even though I'd been abandoned, I had made sure I couldn't be found again. Deep down, I had nurtured my abandonment, allowing myself to justify returning home, to remain alone, strong and tough. The butcher didn't know where I lived, but I was still afraid he'd manage to find me thanks to his wolfish sense of smell. I wanted to prove to myself, and I had done so, that I could be alone in the world. Thinking of his frailty made me fear the butcher even more. Everyone knows that wild animals bite when frightened, and I was afraid of finding him blocking my path once more.

His voice intruded one spring night, so vivid that for a moment I believed he was there. I sat up in bed, staring into the void the words were coming from. We talked at length, like we'd never done before. In the end, I spoke with difficulty, my tongue thick with sleep. I fell asleep talking, while he was still speaking. It was dawn. When I opened my eyes again, my face was sweaty, my eyes felt empty, my mouth sad. The butcher was a man made of darkness, casting a shadow over everything. I wanted to know if he was the ghost of the living or if I'd hoped enough and, in the end, my curses had worked. Whether alive or dead, he had somehow managed to find me.

*

Teaching became impossible, I was sick with fear and impatience. I held back, to avoid giving in to the tremors that called to me. Every sentence seemed like a magic spell, I was afraid the words spewing from my mouth would cause a catastrophe, teaching Marta that a voice can build, but especially destroy, the world. The temptation for obscenity scratched my throat and threatened me to the point of leaving me mute. I didn't want Marta to discover the curses, to become one of us.

But Marta already was. I fearfully listened to her speak in her open way, fearless, displaying a confidence that I'd never been able to exercise freely, and it pierced me mercilessly, leaving me bleeding with envy from deep cuts. Magnificently aggressive, she knew no revenge or resentment because she didn't need them.

"*Devour*, for example, is a beautiful word, it clearly explains what you're saying the moment you pronounce it. You can feel the sound animals make when they open their mouths to scare you," she said. It was her favorite word, she told me, and she would always write to devour what was different from her, to make it her own. She made jokes, raising her arms, bending them toward me. She roared in my face and then laughed heartily. She didn't want to miss anything, she explained, stroking my cheek.

I thought with horror that if Marta had lived in another time, they would have burned her alive, even just because she shamelessly exhibited such dark eyes. I'd always gotten along better with adults, with people who were older than me. Marta was the exception. Marta was a woman yet she was also a male, because she had all the flaws of men. She had a hunter-like quality that recalled my butcher: she knew she could get what she wanted. Like him, she didn't admit cracks nor weaknesses. She lived magic in broad daylight, openly declaring to everyone how she wanted reality to be. She suffered no fear or uncertainty because she let go, willpower coursing through her to open up to things, earning small daily victories. Faced with courage I'd never had and skills I didn't possess, she made me understand the fear people feel in the presence of a strong *fimmina*. If we're not capable, neither can others be.

And yet she wasn't a male. Unlike the butcher, Marta wanted me to be resilient, casting hooks which, after piercing me, could pull out my soul through my throat. Marta wanted me to be limitless; she taught me to explode.

Though I struggled to write, for the first time, I managed nonetheless to feel myself. I was definitely no longer the one giving lessons. I released all my energy, as if it were a bodily need. I allowed myself to feel powerful.

*

Throughout my life, I'd always brooded, and I was accustomed to the shadow and to hiding. Whatever it was, now it wanted to emerge. My torment was no longer a private baseness, it pushed to come out and offend; it wanted to make noise. Anger mounted, and every movement became impatient. My pulse fluttered; my ankles danced when I sat down, I couldn't stay still when I stood up. I returned to tormenting the medallion I'd never taken off. I skinned carcasses and thought of him; I chopped them into pieces and thought of him; I pounded meat and thought of him; I ground remains and thought of him. My headache was back with me.

If knives sank in slowly, it was premeditation and vengeance; sometimes I was blind rage and shredded a mess of scraps, good enough only for the dogs. When I was irritated, I cleaned thoroughly and organized, to avoid succumbing to the paralysis of nameless, reasonless anxiety. I clenched my hands tightly into fists for fear that my flaming soul might slip through my fingers. I no longer hoped nor feared that my curses would have an effect on the world; my consciousness was the world, and I governed it with intent.

What is magic if not the fact that things respond to you, do what you ask of them? Everything around me was an affirmation. My right to be angry was corroborated by the room full of machinery; the heat inside nodded, churning my stomach. Sometimes I spent the night in the back of the shop, to be close to the viscous fumes that nourished my muscles like sap.

Thus two things were happening, seemingly irreconcilable and perhaps actually so, like complementary objects, opposites that coexist and complete each other. I was losing my independence once more; I was becoming stronger because I was now the same as the land.

I was to be feared, and my table and tools knew it before anyone else. Prey to long and frequent bouts of malicious boredom, I'd lose myself in a confusion packed with violent thoughts, followed by a deliberate catalepsy to rest and release my limbs. Overflowing with spite, I destroyed a gnarled wooden cutting board, striking it repeatedly and forcefully until it shattered into splinters and sawdust. I didn't make a sound, except for the involuntary breaths that escaped as I contracted muscles and bones. I felt visited by a brute force, which was nothing but my own. I had long silenced it, but it was nothing but me.

Like in the past, thoughts of the butcher stole my time, occupied my days, haunted my nights. They took me away from my aunt, from Liborio, from Marta. I wasn't writing to Catena. What would he find if he came to look for his wife, to reclaim his tulip? Far from civilized society, miles from America, a cultured life was no longer of any use to me, and I didn't know what I'd become. I didn't put on a show; it's hard to think about it in a place devoid of opportunities. I didn't have to achieve anything, didn't have to go anywhere, didn't have to raise anyone. Trapped in the present, I had no future, and it was probably the best thing that had ever happened to me. With no other pressure than the one from within, it was me, a dense, fickle matter, dynamic, that has no need of definition. If I thought about family, I thought about my aunt; if I thought about connections, I thought about Catena; if I thought about happiness, I thought about Marta, our unexpected, fresh, and splendid meeting. The butcher no longer had the right contours to fit into my life. All that was left for me was to reject him, to break him into pieces, if possible.

I dreamed of earth, damp and porous, and my hands plunging eagerly into it, untangling the homes of worms and the roots of weeds. I shouted, as if to send a signal, slicing through the deserted fields with a sharp voice, terrorizing birds and small animals, keeping emptiness and silence awake. I myself was the dry and stubborn weed that worms its way in and steals space from everything else, never dying. Upon waking, I sometimes found myself unable to leave home, sitting on the threshold, attached to the stone step, the last one you cross before entering. This annoyance was almost as painful as the dirt that lodged itself forcefully between skin and fingers, but I couldn't stop, thinking that this time my mother couldn't stop me either, yelling to demand my presence and call me back to order. I banished order from my spaces. Instead, they housed a creative force that I learned from my aunt, that drove you crazy if you resisted it and that strengthened you if you let go of it.

In the rush of a sweaty night, I even dreamed of my parents, after almost thirty years of not seeing them face to face. I dreamed I was awake and had a tongue made of sand. Anna was holding Papa close and telling me that she'd forgiven me for having come into the world, landing in her house without warning.

*

I couldn't take it anymore. One morning, I woke up with an unbearable restlessness in my body and the need to get away. I hadn't opened the shop in days, the town was out of meat, the smell of blood had started to nauseate me and infest my mind. I waited at the edge of a dark dirt path, sitting on the straw chair I'd dragged from the clearing outside my house, the one my aunt would sit on to weave her baskets. I'd brought it with me by grabbing it by the backrest, and it followed me without squeaking or complaining, bending to my will until I felt I'd found the right spot. The wooden legs sank into the clods, leaving marks behind like a kind of plowing, the only sign of silent resistance. Immersed in a white, pitiless light, I was looking for shadows, my own or those of others, even just of plants or objects, to rest my eyes and relax my spirit. I was alone, the only living thing in the scorched, black, raging countryside, a coal just saved from the fire.

I peeled a fragrant tangerine, which I devoured in a few greedy bites. The peel clung to it tightly, like skin. It took me a few minutes to find the spot where I could break through, enter it. Once I succeeded, I pushed too hard and hurt it. I watched the juice trickle down to my elbow, waiting for it to dry and become sticky. I cut the rough peel into small strips, like my mother used to, enjoying the scent soaking into my fingers. Every now and then, I squinted because of the acidic sprays beading my eyelashes. I delighted in being able to take on a sloppy, disheveled pose. In the middle of nowhere, among barren fields, on the edge of a path that seemed to have neither a beginning nor an end, I was behaving badly. Once again, boredom. I waited, not knowing exactly for what or whom. I waited for the day to turn into evening and then into night, wondering if I'd stay there until morning.

I imagined looking at myself from the outside. I saw a woman from my village, though I didn't feel that old. I'd arranged my raven curls, now streaked with gray, into a thick braid, and I wore a black dress that had belonged to my aunt. The neckline was more generous than those my mother allowed herself, revealing the curves of my breasts, my dark skin beaded with sweat. Another indulgence, fanatical and inappropriate, was a wooden hairpin in shades of gold and green, securing the knots of my hairdo just above my nape.

I had lost myself in the thought that I'd have liked a white dress, the relief of a breeze. I waited, looking around aimlessly. Curious about a large black lava stone, I bent down to pick it up and started stroking it. I wonder how it had rolled all the way from the *Muntagna*. I smoothed it with my fingers; it was almost hot, like me. I let myself absorb it, feeling light, as if I'd started to float in mid-air. Instead, I sank my feet into the sparse, dry grass, into the soil, among the fresh worms I knew so well. I remembered they were alive too.

As the sun began to set, I was about to leave when I saw a man approaching further down the path. Something about his gait unsettled me; I thought it would unsettle anyone. Maybe he leaned slightly to one side. I stood up slowly, the stone clenched in my fist involuntarily, spinning it from right to left between my fingers. And then from left to right, endlessly, as if it were a way to count the minutes. When the man had drawn close, he stopped to look at me. He wasn't from around here. His face was extraordinarily ordinary and unusually clean. No matter how much you wash, the constantly blowing wind lifts and releases dust. If one of us in this region wiped a handkerchief on our forehead to dry it from fatigue, it invariably registered a trace of a dark brown halo.

The thought quickly crossed my mind that it might have to do with the butcher and that I might not recognize him. His age and height matched. I couldn't hold back a chuckle, unexpectedly sharp and shrill. The idea that I might have forgotten him thrilled me. In his eyes, instead, I noticed a hesitation that ruined my fun. I would have been afraid to meet a man alone in a land I didn't know. He liked knowing he didn't need to fear me; I faced a gaze that fears nothing because it knows it can handle everything. He hesitated again, on the point of coming toward me. Instead, he decided to walk away without saying a word. Without even greeting me, he left. Before he turned away, I managed to catch a look of disappointment on his face. He looked at me with amused contempt, mocking me. He had dismissed me, surely thinking I wouldn't be capable, although I still didn't understand of what. He knew what one must desire, how to live and how to live properly.

I was still standing there, my feet dirty, when I made my decision. I started to follow him, picking up my pace. I struck him on the back of his head, with all the strength I could muster, as if it were nothing. I liked the dull sound it made. I smiled, satisfied with and astonished by myself. The man collapsed to the ground and turned over, his wide-open eyes staring at me in disbelief. His reaction offended me and forced me to furrow my brow; I wasn't finished. I crouched over his aching body and began to hit him again and again and again. Pino held my hand steady, helped me hit harder, told me to do it like with the lizards. The stranger was dying between my legs, but I continued, strong. So reckless as to be clear-sighted, more than I'd ever been. Blood covered my hands and wrists, had splattered messily on my arms, thighs, neck, and face, joined my hair in still-warm clots. It was like I wanted to get *rintra*.

I stopped when I could no longer punish him, wiping away a lock of hair glued to my mouth by blood with the back of the hand holding the stone. I felt my strength failing, allowed myself a few minutes to breathe deeply and calm my heart, straddling my prey. I stood up to observe him. He stared blankly at the sky in front of him, not seeing it. I had scared him to death.

I looked around: I couldn't leave him where he was. I grabbed him by the ankles and dragged him away from the path where we'd met just a short while ago, where he had crossed his fate and I mine. Our lives, a pair of scissors that meet at one point and then diverge, in opposite directions but impossible to separate. Everything happens because someone has decreed it so; chance is made up of a dense series of specific decisions and thus does not exist. Every single step fits together perfectly. Everything happens because it had to happen that way; we choose a part, everything else chooses the rest. He had no reason to pass through there except that he knew it was the right path. I had no reason to wait on the same path except that I felt like I had to wait. That day he had to die, and I had to kill; everything and everyone had led us there. And if everything had led us to that moment, it had to happen so it would be followed by what was necessary. So that I could be myself and he would stop being himself and become worms and water and tender sprouts, and maybe even a lemon in the hand of another child, like in the beginning, mixed with our dead countryside. A butcher who becomes butchered meat, allowing himself to be devoured.

I was panting from his weight, helping myself by shouting with effort and liberation as I dragged him toward the wheat fields, among the tall stalks. I would have liked to ask for someone's help, I knew that Marta would have undoubtedly agreed, but she didn't come, she couldn't hear me. I don't know how long we continued, me in a bath of sweat and blood, him so tired, his arms dirty with earth stretched above his head, almost as if surrendering. I finally abandoned him when it seemed we were far enough. No one would look for him, only the animals who'd hide him from the village's eyes, digesting him.

I didn't kill out of hatred or resentment. My heart was stung by an infected insect, a rabid dog's anger took me from that moment and devoured me intimately. That's why I attacked him and wanted to tear him to pieces. No other reason. It's him, I thought. I made him into pulp, just to try it, feeling no scandal in my heart. Just out of curiosity.

When I crossed the threshold of the house, my aunt looked at me silently. With open arms, I approached her, asking for help like a cat that has just given birth and is looking for shelter and comfort. We remained silent while she drew a bath for me in the old-fashioned way, in a metal basin. She helped me undress and carefully folded my dress, as if she'd just taken it from under the sun. I slowly immersed myself in the warm, soapy water, leaning back. I let her wash the blood off me with a soft sponge, detangling and cleaning my hair. For a moment, I felt like a young bride preparing for the altar. I kept my eyes fixed ahead, thinking that I was alive and warm and he was dead and cold.

My aunt didn't ask, and I didn't tell her. Neither she nor anyone else ever knew anything. That evening, she rubbed my skin with love, like my mother never had. I felt good, I was free. I wanted to close my eyes. I closed them thinking of Marta. Of her sharp, sweet shoulder blades. The next day I'd reopen the shop, I'd write to Catena. From then on, I would live in the absolute present, with no future.

I have an old soul, as deep and black as a well; who knows what I'm hiding in there. I'm afraid of the dark, even if I carry it within me. I'm as rough as my origins, which, deep down inside, I haven't completely forgotten. Maybe that's why I like to watch the night in my room. I'm a woman as old as time, I tell stories, I like their sounds; they squeeze your bones as well as your heart. It doesn't matter if they're true or not; at least a part of them always is. And how does this story end? *Comu finisci si cunta*: as it ends, so it is told .

My name is Lucia.

About the Author

SOFIA PIRANDELLO (Rome, 1993) lives and works in Milan. She is the author of the novels *Candido suicida* (Round Robin, 2018) and *Bestie* (Round Robin, 2022), and of *Fantastiche presenze. Note su estetica, arte contemporanea e realtà aumentata* (Johan & Levi, 2023). In 2023, *Bestie* won the SIAE award "Per Chi Crea."

CROSSINGS
An Intersection of Cultures

Crossings is dedicated to the publication of Italian language literature and translations from Italian to English.

Rodolfo Di Biasio. *Wayfarers Four*. Translated by Justin Vitello. 1998. ISBN 1-88419-17-9. Vol 1.

Isabella Morra. *Canzoniere: A Bilingual Edition*. Translated by Irene Musillo Mitchell. 1998. ISBN 1-88419-18-6. Vol 2.

Nevio Spadone. *Lus*. Translated by Teresa Picarazzi. 1999. ISBN 1-88419-22-4. Vol 3.

Flavia Pankiewicz. *American Eclipses*. Translated by Peter Carravetta. Introduction by Joseph Tusiani. 1999. ISBN 1-88419-23-2. Vol 4.

Dacia Maraini. *Stowaway on Board*. Translated by Giovanna Bellesia and Victoria Offredi Poletto. 2000. ISBN 1-88419-24-0. Vol 5.

Walter Valeri, editor. *Franca Rame: Woman on Stage*. 2000. ISBN 1-88419-25-9. Vol 6.

Carmine Biagio Iannace. *The Discovery of America*. Translated by William Boelhower. 2000. ISBN 1-88419-26-7. Vol 7.

Romeo Musa da Calice. *Luna sul salice*. Translated by Adelia V. Williams. 2000. ISBN 1-88419-39-9. Vol 8.

Marco Paolini & Gabriele Vacis. *The Story of Vajont*. Translated by Thomas Simpson. 2000. ISBN 1-88419-41-0. Vol 9.

Silvio Ramat. *Sharing A Trip: Selected Poems*. Translated by Emanuel di Pasquale. 2001. ISBN 1-88419-43-7. Vol 10.

Raffaello Baldini. *Page Proof*. Edited by Daniele Benati. Translated by Adria Bernardi. 2001. ISBN 1-88419-47-X. Vol 11.

Maura Del Serra. *Infinite Present*. Translated by Emanuel di Pasquale and Michael Palma. 2002. ISBN 1-88419-52-6. Vol 12.

Dino Campana. *Canti Orfici*. Translated and Notes by Luigi Bonaffini. 2003. ISBN 1-88419-56-9. Vol 13.

Roberto Bertoldo. *The Calvary of the Cranes*. Translated by Emanuel di Pasquale. 2003. ISBN 1-88419-59-3. Vol 14.

Paolo Ruffilli. *Like It or Not*. Translated by Ruth Feldman and James Laughlin. 2007. ISBN 1-88419-75-5. Vol 15.

Giuseppe Bonaviri. *Saracen Tales*. Translated Barbara De Marco. 2006. ISBN 1-88419-76-3. Vol 16.

Leonilde Frieri Ruberto. *Such Is Life*. Translated Laura Ruberto. Introduction by Ilaria Serra. 2010. ISBN 978-1-59954-004-7. Vol 17.

Gina Lagorio. *Tosca the Cat Lady*. Translated by Martha King. 2009. ISBN 978-1-59954-002-3. Vol 18.

Marco Martinelli. *Rumore di acque*. Translated and edited by Thomas Simpson. 2014. ISBN 978-1-59954-066-5. Vol 19.

Emanuele Pettener. *A Season in Florida*. Translated by Thomas De Angelis. 2014. ISBN 978-1-59954-052-2. Vol 20.

Angelo Spina. *Il cucchiaio trafugato*. 2017. ISBN 978-1-59954-112-9. Vol 21.

Michela Zanarella. *Meditations in the Feminine*. Translated by Leanne Hoppe. 2017. ISBN 978-1-59954-110-5. Vol 22.

Francesco "Kento" Carlo. *Resistenza Rap*. Translated by Emma Gainsforth and Siân Gibby. 2017. ISBN 978-1-59954-112-9. Vol 23.

Kossi Komla-Ebri. *EMBAR-RACE-MENTS*. Translated by Marie Orton. 2019. ISBN 978-1-59954-124-2. Vol 24.

Angelo Spina. *Immagina la prossima mossa*. 2019. ISBN 978-1-59954-153-2. Vol 25.

Luigi Lo Cascio. *Othello*. Translated by Gloria Pastorino. 2020. ISBN 978-1-59954-158-7. Vol 26.

Sante Candeloro. *Puzzle*. Translated by Fred L. Gardaphe. 2020. ISBN 978-1-59954-165-5. Vol 27.

Amerigo Ruggiero. *Italians in America*. Translated by Mark Pietralunga. 2020. ISBN 978-1-59954-169-3. Vol 28.

Giuseppe Prezzolini. *The Transplants*. Translated by Fabio Girelli Carasi. 2021. ISBN 978-1-59954-137-2. Vol 29.

Silvana La Spina. *Penelope*. Translated by Anna Chiafele and Lisa Pike. 2021. ISBN 978-1-59954-172-3. Vol 30.

Marino Magliani. *A Window to Zeewijk*. Translated by Zachary Scalzo. 2021. ISBN 978-1-59954-178-5. Vol 31.

Alain Elkann. *Anita*. Translated by K.E. Bättig von Wittelsbach. 2021. ISBN 978-1-59954-170-9. Vol 32.

Luigi Fontanella. *The God of New York*. Translated by Siân E. Gibby. 2022. ISBN 978-1-59954-177-8. Vol 33.

Kossi Komla-Ebri. *Home*. Translated by Marie Orton. 2022. ISBN 978-1-59954-190-7. Vol 34.

Leopold Berman. *The Story of a Jewish Boy*. Translated by Giuliana Carugati. 2022. ISBN 978-1-59954-192-1. Vol 35.

Alain Elkann. *Nonna Carla*. Translated by K.E. Bättig von Wittelsbach. 2021. ISBN 978-1-59954-201-0. Vol 36.

Luigi Pirandello. *Man, Beast, and Virtue*. Translated by Alice Roche. 2024. ISBN 978-1-59954-205-8. Vol 37.

Maria Teresa Cometto. *Emma and the Angel of Central Park*. 2023. ISBN 978-1-59954-157-0. Vol 38.

Alain Elkann. *A Single Day*. Translated by K.E. Bättig von Wittelsbach. 2024. ISBN 978-1-59954-211-9. Vol 39.

Elisabetta Rasy. *The Indiscreet*. Translated by Siân E. Gibby. 2024. ISBN 978-1-59954-212-6. Vol 40.

Joseph Bathanti. *Sempre Fidele*. Translated by Marina Morbiducci and Darcy Di Mona. 2024. ISBN 978-1-59954-224-9. Vol 41.